"How da[...]
voice u[...]
you presume to take me to task! It is your
conduct which is in question, ma'am, not
mine."

"Not at all!" she flashed. "You are questioning my conduct. I choose to question
yours!"

"You choose?" Incredulity blended with
anger in his voice. "By God, madam! Do
you imagine the fact that you are to become my wife gives you the right to sit in
judgment upon me?"

"If it does, my lord, that is a right which I
will gladly relinquish along with all claim
upon you. Pray oblige me by sending a
notice to the newspapers that our engagement is at an end."

"I shall do nothing of the kind. I do not
intend that you shall make me look a
bigger fool than you have done already."

"Oh, I can claim no credit for that, sir!
Your lordship has achieved it very ably
without my help."

THE
SILVER
NIGHTINGALE

Sylvia Thorpe

FAWCETT CREST • NEW YORK

A Fawcett Crest Book
Published by Ballantine Books
Copyright © 1974 by Sylvia Thorpe

Library of Congress Catalog Card Number: 74-84342

ISBN 0-449-23379-0

Manufactured in the United States of America

First Fawcett Crest Edition: October 1974
First Ballantine Books Edition: February 1989

The
Silver Nightingale

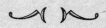

Chapter I

Mrs. Lorymer, informed as she rose from the breakfast table that her eldest son had called to see her on a matter of great urgency, received the news with mingled astonishment and misgiving. Astonishment because Mr. Peregrine Lorymer rarely left his bed, let alone his lodging, before noon; and misgiving because the only thing she could think of urgent enough to cause him to break this habit was a sudden and catastrophic worsening of the state of permanent financial crisis in which he lived.

She dissembled her feelings, however, for she was conscious of the fact that her elder sister, Eliza Gundridge, at whose house in Brook Street she was at present a guest, was looking at her in a commiserating way. Mrs. Lorymer had no wish to be pitied, nor did she see any necessity for it. She doted on her two handsome, heedless sons, Peregrine and Charles, and could only regret that Providence had not seen fit to be as generous to them with material possessions as with looks and charm. Eliza might boast that her own son, George, had never caused her one moment's anxiety in all his twenty-seven years, but Mrs. Lorymer, looking upon that stolid and decidedly tedious young man, felt that there could be too high a price to pay for such peace of mind.

When she entered the drawing room where her firstborn awaited her, she was relieved to see that he appeared to be in the best of spirits; even, in fact, to be labouring under some kind of suppressed excitement. He saluted her with a flourish, told her that she was wearing a devilish becoming cap, and then, when she had seated herself beside the fire, took up a position on the opposite side of the fireplace, and looked down at her with a sparkle of triumph in his eyes.

"Well, Mama," he informed her, "you've done it! Let me be the first to congratulate you."

"Congratulate me?" She was bewildered. "Upon what, my dear boy?"

"On knowing exactly what you were about when you insisted on giving Sal her chance in London before bringing Amy out. I admit I thought you were wasting the ready, but by Jupiter! I was wrong."

"Peregrine!" Mrs. Lorymer sat up straighter, eyeing him hopefully. "Am I to understand that your sister Sarah has received an offer of marriage?"

"She has indeed!"

"Thank Heaven!" she exclaimed devoutly. "Sarah is a dear, good girl and no mother ever had a better daughter, but I will confess to you, Perry, that there have been times when I wondered if I had been foolish in being so scrupulously just. Of course, as the eldest of your sisters it was only proper that she should have a chance to establish herself creditably before I launch Amy into society, and if poor Papa had lived, she would have come out two seasons ago, but even so—! However, all has come right in the end. She has done far better than she could have hoped to do at home in Hampshire, for Mr. Denton possesses a respectable fortune, and is a very good sort of man besides—"

"It's not Denton who has offered for her, Mama," Peregrine interrupted. "It's Chayle."

His mother, brought to an abrupt halt, stared at him with her mouth unbecomingly open and her handsome eyes threatening to start from her head. After a few stunned seconds she murmured in a shaken voice:

"I must have misunderstood you. I thought for a moment you said that Lord Chayle had offered for your sister."

"I did say so, though I don't wonder you didn't believe it. Didn't believe it myself at first. Little Sal, of all people, catching the biggest prize on the Marriage Mart."

His mother was too overcome to rebuke him for this vulgarity. When she had brought Sarah on an extended visit to her Aunt Eliza in London, she had had very little real hope of anything coming of it. For one thing, it was midwinter, when the town was always very thin of company, and for another,

Sarah was the only one of the seven Lorymer children to inherit none of her parents' outstanding good looks—a grave disadvantage for a young lady whose family resources could provide only the most modest marriage-portion. Not that Sarah was really plain; she only appeared so by contrast with her unusually handsome brothers and sisters, and particularly with the dazzlingly beautiful Amy, upon whose success the hopes of the entire Lorymer family had hitherto been pinned.

Yet Sarah, twenty years old, with no advantages and certainly without making the least push to do so, had now won a proposal of marriage from a wealthy nobleman at whom, for years, caps had been set in vain. Her mother could not understand it, nor did she even try. One did not seek to understand miracles; one simply accepted them, with awe and profound gratitude.

"Lord Chayle!" she said reverently. "My little Sarah a baroness! Peregrine, when did he approach you?"

"This morning. When I got home last night I found a note from him, saying he would wait upon me at ten o'clock. (Good thing he sent it, or he'd have found me still abed.) Gave me quite a shock, I can tell you, for I wondered what the devil he wanted. I mean, I've never been closely acquainted with him, and to have him calling on me was something I didn't expect. Didn't expect him to offer for Sal, either. Thought never even crossed my mind."

"You gave your consent, of course?" Mrs. Lorymer prompted with a touch of anxiety.

"Gave my consent? I dashed near fell on his neck," retorted her irrepressible son. "Oh, don't worry, Mama! I said everything that was proper, and then as soon as he had gone, came straight to tell you. Chayle means to call on you this afternoon."

"Sarah must be told at once," Mrs. Lorymer said with decision. "Ring the bell, Perry, so that I may send for her, for I believe she intends to drive out with your cousin Carrie this morning."

He obeyed, and there was a pause while they waited for a servant to come, both mother and son being absorbed in pleasurable contemplation of the sudden and unlooked-for improvement in the family's prospects. When the message to Sarah had been despatched, however, Mrs. Lorymer roused herself to remark:

"I still find it almost impossible to believe. Chayle, I dare say, could have taken his pick of any debutante of the past six or seven seasons, girls of beauty and fortune, so why in the world should he choose Sarah? It cannot be—can it?—that he has become enamoured of her?"

Peregrine gave a crack of laughter scarcely complimentary to his sister. "Shouldn't think so for a moment, ma'am. Sal's hardly in his usual style."

"No, and she has never made the smallest attempt to capture his interest," Mrs. Lorymer agreed perplexedly. "Quite the reverse, in fact. I have noticed an unusual degree of reserve in her manner when in Lord Chayle's company."

A shadow of alarm crossed Peregrine's face.

"Not likely to cast any rub in the way, is she, Mama?"

Mrs. Lorymer shook her head. "Sarah," she said firmly, "knows her duty, and besides, what possible objection could she have? Chayle is more than eligible in every way. She is more fortunate—I will not say than she *deserves*, but than she had any right to hope for. Than any of us had any right to hope for."

"That's true enough," Peregrine agreed with feeling. "As to why he has offered for her, I was thinking about that on my way here, and do you know what I think, ma'am? For years he has had every marriageable girl thrust into his way as soon as she has made her curtsy to society, until he must be heartily bored with the whole business—but you never tried to bring Sal to his notice."

"Only because I thought it would be not the least use," his mother confessed frankly. "I will admit to you, Perry, that I had made up my mind to do everything in my power to set Amy in his way when I bring her to London. But you may be right."

"I'll lay odds I am! *You* never tried matchmaking, and Sal herself hasn't been languishing after him as so many of 'em do. Depend upon it, the last thing Chayle wants is a wife who is forever hanging upon his arm, demanding attention. After all, he's not likely to—!"

Peregrine's exposition of this interesting theory was brought to an abrupt halt at this point by the arrival of his sister. Sarah Lorymer was a petite brunette, with curly dark hair and large, expressive brown eyes, but these assets were, unfortunately, offset by a tip-tilted nose, a wide (though well-shaped) mouth, and a complexion of faintly olive tint which was not flattered by the insipid pastel colours considered proper for a debutante. She greeted her brother with a look of lively astonishment and a demand to be told what might be wrong, to bring him abroad so early.

"Nothing is wrong, my love. Quite the reverse," Mrs. Lorymer replied before Peregrine could speak. She rose and held out her arms. "Come here, my dearest child, and let your mother be the first to felicitate you."

Sarah submitted with docility to the maternal embrace, but across Mrs. Lorymer's shoulder cast an anxiously inquiring glance at her brother. Peregrine, she noticed, was regarding her with affection, which was normal, and also with respectful approval, which was not.

"Dark horse, ain't you, Sal?" he said with a grin. "I would have put *my* money on Amy, but for once I'm dashed glad to have picked the wrong filly. You're a good little soul, and deserve your good luck."

"Peregrine, *must* you talk in that odiously vulgar way?" his mother protested, but in her present mood of well-being the rebuke lacked force. "Not that I disagree with you. Sarah does deserve her good fortune."

"Pray, Mama, tell me what has happened," Sarah entreated, freeing herself from Mrs. Lorymer's hold. "I collect that I have been fortunate enough to receive an offer of marriage, and though I am deeply thankful that the expense of bringing me to London has not been wasted, I do not see why you should be cast into such transports because Mr. Denton wishes to marry me. You *did* expect him to offer, did you not?"

"You may put Mr. Denton out of your thoughts, my love." With an airy gesture, Mrs. Lorymer disposed of the gentleman upon whom, until now, all her hopes for Sarah had depended. She paused impressively, then added with due deliberation: "This morning your brother gave *Lord Chayle* permission to address you. He is coming this afternoon to make you a formal offer."

Sarah stared at her with dilated eyes, going so white that Mrs. Lorymer made haste to clasp an arm about her and guide her to the sofa. Sitting down beside her and briskly chafing her hands, she went on:

"I do not wonder that you are upset, my child, for it is of all things the most unexpected. I should have broken the news to you less abruptly."

"I am quite all right, Mama," Sarah assured her faintly, looking again at Peregrine. "Perry, if this is one of your abominable hoaxes—!"

"Sal!" he exclaimed reproachfully. "No, really, m'dear girl, would I hoax you on such a matter? It's true, give you my word."

"Of course it is true. Peregrine knows better than to jest on a subject which means so much to us all. Now, my love, we must give some thought to what you shall wear to receive Chayle this afternoon. I think the pale pink muslin is the most—"

"Mama, please!" Sarah exclaimed beseechingly. "I have not yet had time—! *Why* should Lord Chayle offer for me? He has never paid me the least attention beyond the ordinary. Why, he does not even like me!"

"Dash it all, Sal, he must like you!" Peregrine expostulated. "Fellow wouldn't offer for a female he disliked."

"I do not mean that he *dis*likes me. He is scarcely aware of my existence."

"Calm yourself, my love," Mrs. Lorymer said firmly. "This news has thrown you into a very natural agitation, but you are being foolish beyond permission. Perry, my dear, I wish that you will go now. I have a great deal to discuss with your sister."

"Going at once, ma'am," he assured her promptly. "Lord, what a morning! *I* hardly know whether I'm on my head or my heels, so it's no wonder Sal's in such a state."

"And, Perry," his mother warned him, "it will not do for you to say anything of this matter to anyone for the present. In due course Lord Chayle will cause a notice of the engagement to be sent to the newspapers."

"No need to fret over that, ma'am. I won't say a word, not even to Charlie." He chuckled. "I'll lay odds, though, that there will be some long faces when the news does become known."

He then prepared to take his leave, but paused to look rather hard at his sister. A little colour had returned to her cheeks, but something in her expression prompted him to ask:

"No objection to Chayle, have you, Sal? You know that neither Mama nor I would try to persuade you to make a match you dislike, no matter what the worldly advantages."

Sarah started, and looked up somewhat guiltily to meet his gaze. A rather forced smile touched her lips, and she said in a rallying tone: "Now who is being foolish, Perry? How could I have any objection when his lordship's person and manner are such as cannot fail to please? I am—just a little overcome, that is all."

"Don't wonder at it, m'dear girl. Floored me, I can tell you, when he told me he wanted to marry you. Thought for a minute he must be foxed."

On this note of brotherly candour he departed, and Mrs. Lorymer, having closely studied her silent daughter for several moments, said gravely:

"Peregrine is right, my child. If you *have* taken Chayle in aversion you must say so now, while there is still time to draw back. I do not wish you to enter into a marriage repugnant to you merely for worldly considerations."

With an effort, Sarah roused herself from her preoccupation. At that moment she would have liked nothing better than to be left entirely alone to consider the overwhelming thing which had befallen her, but it was plain that she was not to be offered this indulgence. Since she was not much accustomed, however, to having her preferences attended to, having been for several years at the beck and call of her parents, brothers and sisters, it did not occur to her to say so. She merely made a determined effort to shake off her abstraction, and said composedly:

"Mama, I do not know Lord Chayle very well, but he has always treated me with the utmost civility, and I certainly do not dislike him. Besides, I hope I know my duty well enough not to whistle so advantageous an offer down the wind. I was prepared, as you know, to accept Mr. Denton should he propose to me, and I am not very well acquainted with him, either."

"What a mercy he did not offer!" Mrs. Lorymer exclaimed involuntarily. "Well, my love, I am glad to find you taking the matter so sensibly, for it might well turn the head of a girl with less than your degree of common sense. I know you will not misunderstand me when I say that it goes far beyond anything I ever hoped for you. Chayle offers you wealth, a title, a position in the first rank of fashion, and will, I feel sure, accord you always every courtesy and consideration. You are very fortunate, Sarah."

"I am very conscious of it, Mama," Sarah replied with a touch of dryness. "In fact, his lordship offers so much that I cannot help wondering why he should offer it to *me*. I am not beautiful, like Amy, or clever or fascinating. I am not even an heiress. There is nothing about me which can possibly have commended me to him."

"There, my dear child, you are very plainly mistaken," her mother pointed out with some amuse-

ment, "and I fancy I can tell you what it is. It cannot have escaped your attention how many young
ladies make no secret of having a *tendre* for him,
and go to such lengths to engage his notice that one
quite blushes for them. You, I am happy to say,
have never done so."

Sarah was looking at her with some dismay. "Do
you mean, Mama, that because I have not flattered
Lord Chayle by seeking to captivate him, he has offered for me out of pique? Oh, surely not!"

"No, no, my love, but I have no doubt that it is
just that little reserve in your manner which has
pleased him. What Chayle will have looked for in
his future wife is not merely that she should be a
modest, well-bred girl who will be a gracious hostess
and a dignified mistress of his household, but, above
all, one who will not embarrass him by forever
hanging upon his sleeve and demanding his company, and enacting tragedies if he does not choose
to bestow it upon her."

"In short," Sarah said bitterly, "a wife who is as
indifferent to him as he is to her. I see!"

Mrs. Lorymer frowned. "Sarah, my child, that
there may be sincere regard between married cou-
ples I do not deny, but that can only come with
time. It is not, I hope, necessary for me to remind
you that a man in Chayle's position does not marry
because he fancies himself to be, in the vulgar
phrase, 'in love'?"

"No, Mama."

"Or that he will expect his wife to be merely

dutiful and submissive, and not to embarrass him and demean herself by any ill-bred display of emotion?"

"No, Mama."

"Nothing," Mrs. Lorymer continued firmly, "would more surely disgust him. Remember that, my child, and conduct yourself towards him with that propriety I have always sought to instil into you. I am convinced that you will. You have never, I am happy to say, been prone to indulge in foolish, romantic fancies, as some girls are."

Sarah's wide, direct gaze remained fixed on her mother's face. "Mama—forgive me, perhaps I ought not to ask such a question—did you not marry Papa because you fell in love with him?"

Mrs. Lorymer sighed. "Yes, child, I did, and *would* have my own way in the matter, even though there were several far more eligible offers for my hand. That is why I have always been firmly resolved that none of my own girls shall make a similar mistake." She saw that Sarah was looking shocked, and added rather sadly: "A romantic attachment, my love, soon fades away when one is constantly in a worry over unpaid bills and the needs of a growing family. You must have realised by now that poor Papa was sadly improvident."

Sarah opened her lips to protest, then closed them again, remembering her childhood in the shabby, rambling old house in Hampshire, the endless economies, the increasingly rare visits of the heedless, pleasure-loving father who had been almost a stranger to his children until at last, incurably ill, he had come home to be nursed devotedly for nearly a year before his death.

"So you see, Sarah," Mrs. Lorymer went on, "though most young girls dream of a love-match, in reality they are far better advised to be guided by their parents in the choice of a husband. I am sure that Lord Chayle will treat you always with kindness and consideration, and as his wife you will be assured not merely of the elegancies of life, but of its luxuries. Remember, too, that you will be in a position to do a great deal for your sisters, and that, I know, is a consideration which must carry weight with you."

She paused, realising that she was talking as though trying to persuade a reluctant daughter to accept an unwelcome suitor, and yet Sarah had shown no reluctance. And, indeed, why should she? Mrs. Lorymer asked herself. She would be acquiring, besides wealth and a title, a very charming and personable husband, and what more could any girl ask? It was absurd to feel that there was any need to persuade Sarah to accept this very flattering offer, so why, Mrs. Lorymer wondered exasperatedly, did she keep urging its many advantages? The shock and excitement, she decided, must have upset her nerves.

Sarah, escaping some twenty minutes later to the privacy she desired, on the pretext of making ready for her drive with Cousin Caroline, closed the door of her bedroom thankfully behind her and walked slowly across to the dressing table. Sitting down, she gazed earnestly at her reflection in the mirror, almost expecting to see some alteration in her appearance. So enormous and unexpected a change in one's prospects ought, surely, to leave its outward mark.

"Lady Chayle," she said softly. "I am going to marry Justin Chayle," but, even spoken aloud, it still lacked reality. One might, while smiling dutifully upon the unexciting Mr. Denton, have woven endless romantic dreams of which his lordship was always the hero, and in which one was never afflicted by the paralysing shyness which, in his actual presence, made one appear so stupid and dull, but to have dreams suddenly transformed into reality was an entirely different matter.

Yet the dreams had not really come true, Sarah reflected miserably. Lord Chayle had offered for her because he wanted a sensible, well-behaved wife who would not make herself tiresome, not because he had fallen in love with her; and she would still be stiff and tongue-tied in his presence, bitterly conscious of the folly of her own feelings and terrified that he might discover them. It would all be quite dreadful, and she wished she could refuse, but how could she, when Mama and Perry had so generously given her the opportunity to do so even though this marriage would mean so much to the whole family? When Mama had been so determined to give Sarah at least a few weeks in town, which she could ill afford with all the expense of Amy's come-out to consider, even though Aunt Eliza and her kind, dull husband had offered hospitality for the entire season? One must do one's duty, but how much easier it would have been to marry Mr. Denton, for whom one felt only the mildest liking, than the man with whom one had fallen so foolishly and completely in love, and who must never, never be allowed to suspect it.

SYLVIA THORPE
22

it would have been to marry Mr. Denton, for whom
one felt only the mildest liking, than the man
who had fallen...

Chapter II

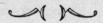

Justin Chayle, tenth Baron Chayle, made ready
for his formal call upon Miss Lorymer in a frame of
mind which reflected his whole attitude to the proposed marriage—resignation to a distasteful duty,
slightly tempered by satisfaction that his choice had
fallen where not even the most avid society gossip
could have foreseen. Peregrine Lorymer had been
right in his supposition that Chayle was heartily
bored by the succession of marriageable girls constantly paraded before him by the tricks and coquet-
ries of the girls themselves, and by their mamas'
endless attempts at matchmaking. In fact, he had
recently passed beyond boredom to the point of
faint disgust.

Justin was twenty-nine years old, and had succeeded to his large inheritance when he was seventeen. He was also the last surviving male of his family, with the exception of an elderly invalid bachelor

cousin living in Harrogate, and he did not need the constant urging of his sisters and aunts to remind him that it was his duty to marry and to provide himself with an heir. Now the prospect of another Season, and another crop of hopeful debutantes, had brought him to the point of making a decision; and a spirit of perversity had caused him to choose the most unlikely of all the eligible young females at that moment available.

There were some, he reflected with a touch of cynicism, who might consider that Sarah Lorymer was not even eligible. Her birth was irreproachable, but her fortune—Justin had taken the trouble to inquire into her family background—nonexistent, while the possession of two expensive elder brothers and four younger sisters must be regarded as liabilities rather than assets. Justin, however, was in the happy position of being able to disregard financial considerations, and in all other respects, he thought, Miss Lorymer would do very well. She was pleasing enough to look at without being a beauty; her manner, quiet and reserved, was totally lacking in coquetry; and she indulged in none of those airs and graces which had begun to set Justin's teeth on edge. She would no doubt bore him as much as any other well-brought-up young girl, but she seemed less likely than her rivals to irritate him.

He was about to leave his house in Mount Street to walk—for the day, though cold, was fine and bright—the short distance to the home of Mr. George Gundridge, M.P., Miss Lorymer's uncle by marriage, when a footman brought him a letter which had just been delivered. His lordship took it from the salver on which it was proffered to him, a faint, impatient frown touching his brow as he recognised the unmistakably feminine hand in which it was addressed. He ripped it open and strolled back to the fire as he glanced through its contents. The frown deepened; he stood for a moment looking at the letter, tapping the faintly perfumed paper with one well-kept fingernail, and then crushed it into a ball and tossed it into the flames. The announcement of his betrothal would, he hoped, put an end to reproaches and importunities from that quarter.

When he arrived in Brook Street, Mrs. Lorymer received him alone in the smaller of the two drawing rooms. It was her moment of triumph. Watching him cross the room towards her, she reflected again how extraordinarily fortunate her daughter was; so brilliant a match, and so personable a husband. Chayle was undeniably handsome—even though, at first glance, his looks might give an impression of coldness, for he had fair hair, cool grey eyes, and a somewhat austere cast of countenance. Yet those eyes could warm quite surprisingly, and he had a smile which could, at times, quite transform his face.

That particularly warm expression was not in evidence as he replied to Mrs. Lorymer's greeting, but she had scarcely expected that it would be, since she was under no illusion regarding his reason for proposing to Sarah, and she hoped that, after their talk that morning, Sarah was not either. When civilities had been exchanged, Chayle said courteously:

"It is good of you to receive me, ma'am. No doubt Mr. Peregrine Lorymer has acquainted you with the reason for my visit?"

"He has, my lord, and I am deeply sensible of the honour you do my daughter."

"May I then assume, ma'am, that my proposal has your approval as well as your son's? I appreciate that he is Miss Lorymer's guardian, but in the circumstances I would be happy to know that you, too, look with favour upon the match."

"My dear sir, how could I do otherwise? The happiness and well-being of a child must always be a mother's first consideration, and Sarah's, I am persuaded, must be safe in your keeping."

"I shall endeavour, ma'am, to ensure that you never have cause to alter that opinion." Justin was beginning to be bored with this polite verbal fencing. "Is it too much to hope that Miss Lorymer is equally complaisant?"

Mrs. Lorymer smiled somewhat archly. "The answer to that question, my lord, you shall have from her own lips. I will desire her to join us."

Sarah, awaiting the expected summons in her room, was by this time in a churning state of nerves, pacing up and down with her hands pressed tightly to her midriff. If only Chayle would come soon, so that she could get the ordeal over while some shreds of composure still remained to her. Mama had promised not to leave her alone with him, but even with this assurance of support Sarah felt miserably certain that much more of this waiting would reduce her to such a state of agitation that she would not be able to conceal it.

Yet when at length the summons came, she would have given anything to defer the meeting a little longer, but, since this was out of the question, she forced herself to walk out of the room and down the stairs. The drawing room, when she reached it, seemed to have grown to enormous proportions, so that she had to cross an endless expanse of floor, conscious all the time of Justin Chayle's gaze upon her and feeling certain that the mere sight of her in such discomposure must cause him to regret the step he had taken.

In point of fact, none of her inner turmoil was visible in her face or bearing; she appeared quite composed, and if her expression was rather serious, well, this was a serious occasion. Had she ventured to look directly at Justin she would have seen that he was regarding her with mild approval, but after one fleeting glance at him, which caused her heart to jump as absurdly as it always did when she saw him, she looked instead at her mother. Mrs. Lorymer had risen from her chair and now came forward to meet her.

"My love," she said fondly, "I have told you of the very flattering offer your brother has received for your hand, but it is only fitting that his lordship should receive his answer from you. That the match has my approval, and Peregrine's, he is already aware."

"It is my hope, Miss Lorymer," Justin said with a smile, which Sarah, eyes downcast, did not see, "that you will allow yourself to be persuaded by the advice of your mother and brother. Will you do me the very great honour of becoming my wife?"

Sarah took a deep breath, and said faintly that she was very much obliged to his lordship and would be happy to accept his proposal, of the honour of which she was deeply sensible. Mrs. Lorymer took her hand and placed it in Justin's. He kissed it, and Sarah, intensely aware of his light, firm clasp and the brief touch of his lips, prayed silently that he would not notice how much her fingers were trembling.

The announcement of the engagement of Sarah Lorymer to Justin Chayle, appearing in the *London Gazette* and other society journals, was quite as great a shock to the Polite World as his lordship had maliciously foreseen. Astonishment, disapproval, and envy greeted it everywhere, but nowhere were these emotions—and others—more keenly felt than in an elegant small house in Half Moon Street, the home of Mrs. Helena Maitland.

This wealthy and opulently beautiful young widow, glancing through the *Gazette* as she lingered over a belated breakfast, saw the announcement and uttered a shriek of rage, which caused her brother Bertram, who shared the house but not its upkeep, to start and shudder with the air of a man undergoing torture.

"Dash it all, Nell! *Must* you squawk like that?"

he demanded faintly. "Told you I'm not feeling quite the thing."

Mrs. Maitland ignored him. Clutching the paper in both hands, she stared at it much as though it were the Gorgon's head, then crushed it furiously into a ball and cast it from her with a gesture of repudiation which sent two plates and a coffee cup crashing to the floor.

"Damn him!" she exclaimed passionately. "Damn him, damn him, *damn* him!" She snatched up the coffeepot and hurled it into the fireplace.

Bertram prudently moved out of her reach the tankard of ale with which he was fortifying himself, then retrieved the *Gazette* and smoothed its crumpled pages. It took him only a moment to find the item which had so disturbed his sister.

"Told you so!" he said gloomily when he had read it. "Setting your sights too high, my girl, that's what you were doing."

"I will not endure it!" she said in a shaking voice. "To be cast aside for that—that dowdy, countrified little nobody. Oh, it is beyond all bearing!"

"Don't know that he's casting you aside," Bertram pointed out reasonably. "Got engaged to Miss Lorymer, that's all. Surprised he hasn't done something of the kind before. Got to think of the succession."

This earned him a look of blasting contempt from his sister's very fine blue eyes. Her face was white with rage, and her magnificent bosom heaved.

"Fool!" she said in accents of loathing. "Drunken fool! My God! Why do I put up with you?"

"Not as big a fool as you, Nell, drunk *or* sober,"
he retorted. "Windmills in your head, my dear girl,
that's what you've got. Told you weeks ago, men of
Chayle's stamp don't marry their mistresses."

She glared at him. He had indeed warned her,
several times, but Mrs. Maitland had as little liking
as anyone for those who said "I told you so."

"No," she said bitterly, "they marry stupid, sim-
pering little bread-and-butter misses like Sarah
Lorymer, with no looks, no countenance, and no
conversation. Mercy on us! What has she to offer
such a man as Justin Chayle?"

"A reputation," Bertram informed her brutally.
"Thing you lost years ago, m'dear, long before old
Maitland slipped his moorings."

Mrs. Maitland leaned across the table towards
him. "Be careful, my dear brother," she said silkily.
"I house and feed you very well, and you are not
indispensable."

"Yes, I am," he replied calmly. "You need me to
lend you countenance and some semblance of respectability. Half the doors in London would be
closed to you if you lived alone, and you know
damned well you couldn't endure a female companion, even if one could be found who would stay
with you." He drained his tankard, tossed aside the
Gazette and rose to his feet. "Spoiled your own
chances, my girl, that's what you did," he added pityingly. "You should have shown a measure of patience once you'd brought old Maitland up to
scratch, instead of playing fast and loose. Stood to

reason the old fellow'd soon get his notice to quit, and a handsome young widow—good breeding, purse well lined—might easily have made a catch like Chayle. As it is—!" He paused, shook his head, and let an eloquent shrug complete the sentence.

Mrs. Maitland turned her back on him.

At another breakfast table not far away, the announcement inspired feelings of a very different kind. Mr. Peregrine Lorymer, having read it three times and found that it did not pall in the least by repetition, finally passed it across to his brother Charles. Both young men were a trifle pale and heavy-eyed, for they had spent most of the previous night celebrating.

Charles studied the announcement in his turn, nodding his satisfaction. "Looks good, don't it?" he remarked. "Lucky for Sal Chayle took a notion to her." He paused, considering. "Lucky for all of us."

"Especially for the other girls," Peregrine agreed. "I dare say Amy would have done well enough, with her looks, but as the sister of Lady Chayle—! Mark my words, Charlie, we'll see *her* wearing a coronet before the year's out."

Charles agreed, merely pointing out, though not in any argumentative spirit, that one very rarely *saw* a peeress actually wearing her coronet. Then, the thought of his second sister leading inevitably to the usual mental comparison between Amy and Sarah, he added:

"You know, Perry, I can't help wondering *why* Chayle picked Sal, when beauties like the Salton girl are languishing after him. I mean, *we* know she's a right 'un, but there's no denying she don't take the eye."

"Perhaps he don't want a wife who takes the eye," Peregrine pointed out reasonably. "Melissa Salton's a beauty, I grant you, but imagine being married to her. She's as jealous as the devil, and I'll lay odds she'll make her husband's life a misery. Mama and I believe that Chayle noticed Sal in the first place because she didn't set her cap at him, and offered for her because he wants a quiet wife who won't make a nuisance of herself."

"A quiet wife," Charles repeated ruminatively. He chuckled. "Going to get a surprise, isn't he, the first time Sal has one of her crazy notions."

His senior regarded him with disfavour. "That's a fine way to talk," he said reprovingly. "Anyone would think Sal was queer in the attic. She only cuts loose a trifle if she loses her temper."

"I know that, but you're not going to tell me, are you, that she'll never lose her temper with Chayle? Bound to, sooner or later."

A reluctant grin crept over Peregrine's face. "As long as it's later rather than sooner. Once they're shackled it won't matter, and in the meantime we can depend on Mama to see that they're not together enough for him to set up Sal's back."

"Dare say you're right," Charles agreed, but there was a faint note of doubt in his voice. "Shouldn't think, though, that Sal would have things all her own way if he did. Chayle's cool enough on the surface, but that sort often have the devil's own temper."

"Won't do any harm," Peregrine said carelessly. "Stop 'em growing bored with each other. After all, it's not as though Sal were a bad-tempered female, quarrelling all the time. It's just that when she does get angry she says and does the first thing that comes into her head, without stopping to think where it may lead."

"That's the trouble," Charles said dubiously. "Not the sort of thing Chayle will like, if you ask me."

"I didn't ask you," Peregrine retorted irritably. "For the Lord's sake, Charlie, stop raising difficulties! Sal's engagement to Chayle is the best thing that ever happened to this family, and don't you forget it."

Sarah herself, in the days which followed, found that the announcement of her engagement had shot her from social obscurity to social prominence. Chayle was punctiliously attentive. He squired her to various functions, and to the theatre; took her driving in the park when the weather was fine; escorted her on duty visits to one or two of his more elderly relatives who lived within easy reach of London. Yet they remained as much strangers to each other as on the day she had accepted his proposal. They were never alone. Sarah's mother or aunt, or Mrs. Gundridge's married daughter, Caroline Blackstead, always accompanied them, or there were servants in close attendance. Justin, though unfailingly courteous, remained aloof, while Sarah, terrified of betraying herself by word or look, became more stiff and tongue-tied than before.

Nor was this the only cross she had to bear, for she was obliged to endure a good deal of backbiting and sweetly smiling malice, not only from other unmarried girls and their mamas but also from those young matrons who, having yearned unavailingly over Justin Chayle in past seasons, were now married to other, less excitingly attractive gentlemen. Even her cousin Caroline could not resist adding a slightly barbed afterthought to her felicitations.

"It is a splendid thing for you, Sarah, and I am heartily glad for your sake, but I cannot help feeling sorry for Amy. So much will now be expected of her. Since *you* have succeeded in fixing Chayle's interest, we shall look to see *her* marry an earl at the very least."

Sarah laughed, for she knew that Carrie meant no real harm, and was, in fact, enjoying the reflected glory of her cousin's triumph, but there were other things less easy to shrug off. The reaction, for instance, of her maternal grandmother, Lady Marlby, with whom she had always enjoyed an especially affectionate relationship. Her ladyship, while applauding the worldly advantages of the match, could wish, she wrote to Sarah from her home in Kent, that the bridegroom was anyone other than Justin Chayle. She had disliked his late mother intensely, for a more deceitful, untrustworthy, arrogant woman she had never known, and it was to be feared that her son closely resembled her. Mrs.

Lorymer, when Sarah showed her the letter with some dismay, told her with a laugh to pay no heed to it. Grandmama's long-standing feud with the late Lady Chayle had for years been a family joke, for it had its beginning in some quite trivial incident which both ladies had eventually forgotten, even though they never forgot the enmity thus aroused. As for Lord Chayle, Grandmama's acquaintance with him was of the slightest, so her judgment of his character was scarcely to be depended upon.

Sarah, reassured, obediently put Lady Marlby's criticisms from her mind until, some three weeks after her engagement, an incident occurred which recalled them forcibly to her mind. She had driven with Carrie to Hookham's Library in Bond Street, which thoroughfare was thronged, as it usually was in the early afternoon, with fashionable people and elegant equipages. The library, too, had its complement of ladies and gentlemen, for it was as much a social meeting place as a dispensary of books, and Sarah and Caroline encountered numerous acquaintances. They were standing among a small group when Helena Maitland came by on the arm of Sir Henry Rossington, a middle-aged roué who was one of her most persistent admirers. All her attention was apparently held by this gentleman, but as she drew level with Sarah's party, they heard her say in a clear, carrying voice:

"My dear Sir Henry, there is no more absurd spectacle than a woman unexpectedly occupying a position in life for which, by custom and accomplishments, she is totally unfitted. Indeed, one would pity such persons if they were not so ridiculous." She paused, gave a start so obviously feigned that it was in itself a mockery, and added quickly: "Why, Miss Lorymer, I did not see you there! You must pay no heed to what I say, my dear. No heed at all."

There was a brief, startled pause, broken by a stifled titter, then several people began to talk at once. Sir Henry, looking appalled, hurriedly directed his companion's attention to someone on the other side of the room, and bore her off in that direction, while Sarah, utterly dumbfounded by an attack as venomous as it was unexpected, stared blankly after them. Her acquaintance with Mrs. Maitland was of the slightest, for though they had been present at a number of the same social events and knew each other's identity, they had never passed beyond the stage of exchanging formal bows. She was therefore completely at a loss and, at first, too astonished to be angry.

It was not until they were once more in Mrs. Blackstead's carriage on their way back to Brook Street that indignation began to get the better of her. She recalled the slighting words, which were all the more wounding for being an echo of some of her own doubts and fears regarding the future, and the sheer malice of the tone in which they had been uttered, and her temper began to stir. Until now she had been too overwhelmed by the change in her prospects, too conscious of her own limitations, to do more than endure with outward composure the veiled gibes directed at her, but Helena Maitland's attack had been the most open as well as the most virulent. It was time, Sarah reflected ominously, that Mrs. Maitland and others like her learned that the future Lady Chayle was not the meek and ineffectual creature they all seemed to suppose.

"It is not to be borne!" she said suddenly, breaking in without apology on her cousin's inconsequential chatter, to which in any case she had not been listening. "I assure you, Carrie, that if Mrs. Maitland makes one more remark of that kind in my hearing, I shall be downright uncivil in return."

"Oh, no, don't do that!" Carrie replied in some alarm. "It is far more dignified to ignore it, you know."

"Ignore it?" Sarah repeated indignantly. "How can one ignore being made an object of ridicule? You heard what she said. She deliberately implied that I am unfitted to be the bride of Lord Chayle. Well, so I may be, but it is not for her to say so!"

"Indeed it is not, and I do not wonder that you are vexed, but it is all spite and jealousy, you know. I do not say her heart is involved, for I am sure she has none, but her ambition has certainly suffered a sad blow. Remember, though, that she makes *herself* look foolish, rather than you, by betraying her absurd pretensions, for her conduct towards you makes it plain that she really did think that Chayle might marry her."

"Chayle—marry Mrs. Maitland?" Sarah said in a stifled voice.

"*She* seems to have thought so," Carrie replied with a laugh, "though one cannot imagine how she could be such a simpleton, when the veriest green-horn knows that a connection of *that* nature does not lead to marriage." She suddenly became aware of a certain rigidity in her companion's bearing, and added uneasily, "You did know about it, Sarah, did you not? Surely my aunt warned you, for she must know that you were bound to hear of it sooner or later."

"Warned me of what, Carrie?" Sarah found that she had to make a considerable effort to speak naturally. "I am not sure that I perfectly understand you."

"Why, about Chayle's liaison with Helena Maitland. Now, Sarah, don't be missish and try to pretend you do not know that such things happen. I know an unmarried girl is supposed to be unaware of such irregular relationships, but when one has brothers like Cousin Peregrine and Cousin Charles —!"

"Of course I know," Sarah interrupted impatiently. "I have heard Perry and Charlie talking of actresses and opera-dancers and what they call 'bits of muslin,' but I never supposed that a lady of quality—!" She paused, frowning. "You speak as though this were a matter of common knowledge."

"Well, of course it is. It was one of the *on-dits* of the town last season, but it is stale news now and no one troubled to remark on it any more until your engagement was announced, and she was unable to conceal her jealousy and resentment."

Sarah was still frowning. "But one may meet her almost anywhere."

"My dear child," Caroline said pityingly, "if such indiscretions led to a woman not being received, half the Polite World would be ignoring one another. It is not, after all, as though Chayle had her in keeping. Her late husband left her very well provided for."

"I do not see that that makes it any better."

"It does not, of course, but there is nothing one can do about it," Carrie said with a sigh. "One must remember that people of quality do not marry for love, and so we are obliged to look the other way if our husbands choose to take a mistress. A wife's position is unassailable, but you will find that there is a price to be paid for it."

There was a note of resignation in her voice which Sarah found intensely irritating, but she made no comment, and Carrie, with unmistakable relief, began to talk instead of the dress-party which Lady Peterby, Chayle's eldest sister, was giving the following evening in honour of the betrothed couple. Carrie was to chaperone Sarah to this, for both Mrs. Lorymer and Mrs. Gundridge were laid low with feverish colds which confined them to bed.

"Such a pity that my aunt is to miss Lady Peterby's party," Carrie was saying, "for she is a notable hostess and the company she gathers together is always brilliant. Lady Bellingham's tonight, too! Of course I am delighted to be taking you, Sarah, but it does seem unjust that your Mama should be obliged to forego all these gatherings when your engagement has just been announced."

Sarah returned some appropriate reply, and Carrie, whose perception was not great, rattled on cheerfully, thankful that the awkward conversation about Helena Maitland was over. Had either Mr. Peregrine or Mr. Charles Lorymer been present, he would have taken instant alarm at sight of his sister's brooding eyes and set lips, but Carrie Blackstead was not sufficiently well acquainted with her cousin to interpret these danger signs. She was not even aware that Sarah had a temper, much less one apt to lead her into reckless and unbecoming behaviour. She was to discover it all too soon for her comfort.

Chapter III

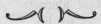

Since it was Mrs. Blackstead who had disclosed the truth, it was perhaps just that she should be accompanying Sarah the next time Miss Lorymer and Mrs. Maitland met. This was only a few hours later, at Lady Bellingham's evening party, an event which her ladyship described as small and informal but which nevertheless brought together some seventy persons of fashion, a fair proportion of whom witnessed an encounter which by the following morning was the talk of the town.

Sarah had spent much of the intervening time brooding over what Carrie had told her. She was deeply hurt, for, unlike Helena Maitland, her heart was involved, and now she could no longer even hope that, since Justin had chosen her from among so many rivals, he must feel some degree of partiality. He felt none; not even kindness towards her, or he would not have exposed her to such humiliation as she had suffered today. All he wanted was a well-bred, self-effacing nonentity, who would be thankful for the wealth and position he could offer her; who would in due course provide him with an heir; and who would not dare object to his amours, even though these were a matter of common knowledge.

While she dressed for the party, in a demure gown of pale blue crepe which, combined with the fact that she was very pale, made her look decidedly sallow, a mental picture of Helena Maitland hovered tormentingly before her eyes. Helena, with the dazzling complexion, golden hair, and magnificent figure which was the same type of beauty as Sarah's own sisters already possessed or gave promise of, and which therefore had always seemed to Sarah the only true yardstick of feminine loveliness. Helena, with the assurance of that beauty, of wealth, of experience. Helena, who was Justin Chayle's mistress.

The anger which had been Sarah's first reaction to that discovery had given way by now to utter misery, and had she been able to follow her present inclination, which was to creep away to some remote but unspecified spot where she need never see Justin, Helena, or any other member of the Polite World again, the temper which no one outside her immediate family suspected her of possessing would probably have remained quiescent. Since such withdrawal was impossible, she finished dressing, looked with acute distaste at her reflection in the mirror, and went downstairs to wait for Carrie, wondering unhappily how she could bring herself to face her betrothed, who would also be present at Lady Bellingham's.

When Carrie arrived she appeared to have forgotten the incident at Hookham's, and this encouraged Sarah, who had felt that everyone she encountered would be laughing at her behind her back, to face the rest of her fellow guests with an appearance, at least, of equanimity. She maintained this tolerably well until, strolling through the larger of Lady Bellingham's salons with Carrie and a gentleman of their acquaintance, a movement of the crowd brought her face to face with Mrs. Maitland, who from her stately height smiled down at her with a kindness as odious as it was false.

"Miss Lorymer! How charming to see you again so soon, and how pretty you look tonight, child, in that delightful gown!"

Sarah looked at her. She was well aware that her own modest attire faded into insignificance by comparison with the daring gown which was making the most of Helena's considerable charms, and the calculated insolence of the greeting, which must be apparent to everyone within earshot, swamped misery with rage, and nudged her irresistibly over the edge of recklessness. Without pausing to consider the consequences, she allowed her gaze to slide indifferently over the other woman from her face to the toes of her satin slippers, and then back to her face again; her brows lifted a fraction, with a disdain that Mrs. Maitland herself could not have equalled, and then, as though Helena did not exist, she resumed her momentarily interrupted conversation with Carrie and Mr. Chilcot.

The whole incident occupied only a matter of seconds, and the stunned silence which succeeded it scarcely longer before the hum of talk broke out again, interspersed now with a few chuckles. Mrs. Maitland stood as though paralysed, while a dark flush of mortification spread upwards over her throat and face to the roots of her beautifully dressed golden hair; she looked as though she could not believe what had happened, any more than she could have believed it if a kitten she had been tormenting had suddenly unsheathed the claws of a tigress.

Sarah enjoyed one exquisite moment of triumph, of pure, unalloyed feminine satisfaction in the total discomfiture of a rival. Then, for the first time, she looked beyond her enemy—into the coldly furious face of Justin Chayle.

His expression made it abundantly plain that he had witnessed her encounter with Mrs. Maitland, and the shock of realising this was so great that Sarah felt the floor heave under her feet. The room seemed to spin round her in a dazzle of light and colour, and from a great distance she heard Carrie exclaim despairingly:

"Oh, mercy! *Now* she's going to swoon. Mr. Chilcot, support her, for heaven's sake!"

Mr. Chilcot, unhappily expostulating, obeyed in a gingerly fashion, but an instant later his tentative clasp was replaced by a ruthlessly firm grip, and Justin's voice said curtly:

"Thank you, Chilcot. You may leave Miss Lorymer in my charge, and her cousin's." Then, in a savage undertone which only Sarah and Carrie could hear, he added: "Pull yourself together! You have done enough harm already, without making a further spectacle of yourself."

She was swept unceremoniously to a chair, while Carrie produced smelling salts from her reticule and agitatedly urged her to make use of them. Sarah sniffed thankfully at their pungent aroma, and her surroundings swam into focus again. The crowded room, the other guests discreetly ignoring her, Carrie hovering distractedly at her side with Justin standing behind her. Sarah stole one glance at his face and said in a choking whisper:

"Oh, Carrie, take me home! I feel dreadfully unwell."

Carrie was given no chance to reply; Justin said smoothly: "There is no need to trouble Mrs. Blackstead. I will take you home."

"No!" Sarah uttered faintly. "Carrie, no!"

"Indeed, my lord," Carrie began diffidently, "do you not think—?"

"No, ma'am, I do not." He spoke courteously, but there was a steely note in his level voice. "I do not believe Miss Lorymer's indisposition serious enough to warrant spoiling *your* pleasure."

Carrie, already thrown off balance by Sarah's behaviour, could find no way of countering this politely phrased command, for such she knew it to be. She looked helplessly from him to Sarah and then at Lady Bellingham, who had joined them during this exchange. Her ladyship responded with a tiny, warning shake of her head.

"I am sure Lord Chayle is right, my dear Mrs. Blackstead," she said soothingly, "and you may quite properly leave Miss Lorymer in his charge, you know." To Sarah she added, not unkindly but with a good deal of meaning: "I am sorry, my child, that you do not feel quite the thing, and it will be far better for you to go home at once. It is what your Mama would wish, I know."

Sarah, abandoned by hostess and chaperone alike, had no choice but to yield to the will of the courteously implacable gentleman at her side, and to get up, place her hand on his proffered arm and, after an incoherent murmur of apology and farewell to Lady Bellingham, allow herself to be led away. Carrie, watching them go, said uneasily:

"Perhaps I should have insisted upon accompanying them."

"That would have been most unwise," Lady Bellingham assured her dryly. "Believe me, my dear, in these circumstances you would have made a very uncomfortable third."

Sarah, handed up into his lordship's carriage, felt quite sick with apprehension, for though Chayle's manner towards her during their departure from the Bellingham house had displayed a proper solicitude, this was totally belied by the look in his eyes, which left her in no doubt of the extent of his anger. As they began to move along the street he said icily:

"Now, perhaps, you will be good enough to tell

me what the devil you mean by behaving as you did just now. Even if you do not know how to conduct yourself, you ought at least to have sufficient common sense not to give rise to gossip by indulging your tantrums."

Words and tone combined to have a curious effect upon Sarah. Guiltily aware that she had not behaved well, she might have been persuaded into an apology if he had taken a more moderate tone, but now her temper flared up again as fiercely as his, so that for the first time in his presence she felt neither shy nor inarticulate.

"I suppose that by giving rise to gossip I am poaching upon your lordship's preserves? I understand that you and Mrs. Maitland have already achieved considerable success in that respect."

He was as astonished by that swift retaliation as Helena had been a short while earlier and for a moment was stunned into silence; but only for a moment.

"How dare you?" he said then, in a low voice unsteady with anger. "How dare you presume to take me to task! It is *your* conduct which is in question, ma'am, not mine."

"Not at all!" she flashed. "*You* are questioning my conduct. *I* choose to question yours!"

"*You* choose?" Incredulity blended with anger in his voice. "By God, madam! Do you imagine the fact that you are to become my wife gives you the right to sit in judgment upon me?"

"If it does, my lord, that is a right which I will

gladly relinquish along with all claim upon you. Pray oblige me by sending a notice to the newspapers that our engagement is at an end."

"I shall do nothing of the kind. It is enough that you have set tongues wagging tonight by your childish tantrums and lack of dignity. I do not intend that you shall make me look a bigger fool than you have done already."

"Oh, I can claim no credit for that, sir! Your lordship has achieved it very ably without my help."

His hand shot out to close about her wrist in a grip that made her gasp. The light in the carriage was very dim but strong enough to let her see that he was smiling. The smile was neither pleasant nor reassuring.

"And with whose aid, ma'am, did you achieve your degree of hoydenish want of conduct? Our engagement stands. I would not for the world forego the pleasure of schooling you."

"I will not marry you!" To Sarah's disgust a tremor of alarm had forced itself into her voice. She knew that Chayle had detected it, for his chilling smile broadened a trifle. "You cannot compel me to do so. I shall tell Mama—!"

"Do so, by all means," he agreed cordially. "I can promise you that you will meet with scant sympathy in that quarter, or from your brother."

She knew, with humiliation, that this was true. She was naturally not familiar with the financial arrangements connected with her forthcoming marriage, but she did know that Chayle had been gen-

erous. It might be true that Mama would not have
forced her unwillingly into the original contract,
but now that the engagement was an accomplished
fact she would never be allowed to withdraw. It was
more likely that she would be punished in some way
for so rashly endangering it.

"Let us pass, therefore," Justin continued coldly,
"to the means by which we may remedy the harm
you have done. Fortunately, since our whole acquaintance will now be waiting eagerly to see how
matters stand between us, tomorrow evening my sister holds her party in our honour. We shall attend
it together, and we shall let it be seen that we are on
the best of terms. That should scotch any rumours
as far as you and I are concerned. For the rest, the
next time you meet Mrs. Maitland you will treat her
with civility. I will undertake to see that you are not
rebuffed."

"Am I expected to be grateful to you for that?
Oh, this is intolerable! Let me tell you, my lord,
that nothing will persuade me to pretend to be on
friendly terms with your—your—!"

"Yes, Miss Lorymer?" Chayle's voice was as
smooth as silk. "With my—what?"

"With your mistress," she flashed, goaded beyond endurance. "For how long did you suppose
you could keep me in ignorance of that?"

"Do you imagine," he replied in a tone of cold
contempt, "that I have felt it necessary to conceal
from you something which concerns you not at all?
You astonish me, Miss Lorymer! That an unmarried

girl of gentle birth should be aware of such matters is deplorable. That she should speak of them is unforgivable."

"Since you find my frankness unforgivable, my lord, it is no doubt just as well that we are not, after all, to be married. I shall, of course, send Lady Peter-by a note first thing in the morning, explaining why I shall not be present at her party, and offering her my apologies."

"Do not be absurd," Justin said coldly. "You are as well aware that such a communication would be disregarded as you are that you will do exactly as I bid you, and when your temper has cooled a trifle you will admit it. You have no choice in the matter, Miss Lorymer. No choice at all." As the carriage slowed and came to a halt in front of Mr. Gundridge's house, he added with infuriating condescension: "We shall say no more about your exceedingly unbecoming remarks. The incident is closed."

She was spared the necessity of replying by the footman opening the door and letting down the steps. Justin assisted her to alight, escorted her to the front door, and bade her a punctilious goodnight. Sarah, acutely conscious of the servant who had opened the door, responded civilly, and the mere fact that she felt obliged to do so brought home to her the inescapable truth of Justin's words. There was absolutely nothing she could do, no course open to her but the humiliating one he had indicated.

She went straight to her room, where she was joined a few minutes later by her abigail, flustered and concerned by this unexpectedly early return. Lucy, who had come with them from Hampshire, was only a year or two older than Sarah, and from the circumstance of her being the daughter of the Lorymers' coachman, they had known each other all their lives. Their relationship was more that of friends than of mistress and maid, and Lucy was devoted to Sarah, whom she considered to be sadly put upon by her heedless brothers and sisters.

"Miss Sarah," she exclaimed now as she hurried into the room, "whatever is the matter to bring you home so early? Don't tell me you've gone and taken Mistress's cold?"

Sarah, who was standing rigidly in the middle of the room with her evening cloak still on and her hands clenched hard on the dainty satin reticule she carried, shook her head impatiently.

"Oh Lucy, don't fuss! I have the headache, that is all."

Lucy, coming forward to take the cloak from her shoulders, cast a shrewd glance at her face, and a look of comprehension came into her own.

"It's not the headache that's ailing you, miss," she said bluntly. "What's happened to put you in such a rage?"

Sarah looked at her with smouldering resentment, but this faded as she met the genuine concern in the abigail's eyes.

"You know me too well, Lucy," she said ruefully. "Yes, I am angry. More angry, I think, than I have ever been in my life—and more humiliated."

She dropped the reticule into Lucy's hands and

begain stripping off her long gloves of soft kid. This
exposed to view the very fine diamond ring which
Chayle had given her to mark their betrothal, and
the sight of the jewel brought all her wrongs before
her again. She dragged it from her finger and flung
it on to the dressing table so violently that it
bounced off again and rolled across the floor. Lucy,
with a gasp of dismay, sprang forward to retrieve it.

"Miss Sarah," she said accusingly as she straightened up with the ring in her hand, "you've quarrelled with his lordship!"

"Quarrelled with him?" Sarah repeated bitterly.
"Oh no, Lucy! One does not quarrel with Lord
Chayle. One is scolded and commanded and treated
with the utmost contempt, all because one dares
object to being publicly humiliated by a woman
whose claim upon his consideration is greater, it
seems, than that of his future wife."

"So that's it!" Lucy said gloomily. "You've found
out about that Mrs. Maitland. I knew it would set
the cat among the pigeons when you did."

Sarah was staring at her in disbelief. "You
knew?" she asked incredulously. "Lucy, how?"

The maid looked troubled. "I've not been prying, miss, if that's what you think. It's just that London servants seem to know more about what goes
on abovestairs than them that lives there, and you
can't help but hear things in a house like this. To
my mind, Mistress should've told you before ever
you gave his lordship an answer, but since she
didn't, it wasn't my place to interfere. But I knew

it would upset you when you did find out. Shameful, I call it!"

"Say 'shame*less*,' Lucy, and you will come nearer to the truth," Sarah retorted with a bleak little laugh. "Well, since you know so much, I had better tell you the rest, and then you will see what good cause I have to be angry. Come, help me out of this hateful dress. I shall go to bed directly."

While Lucy undressed her, she recounted the events of the day and found considerable relief in being able to speak without reserve to someone of whose sympathy she was assured. In this respect Lucy did not disappoint her, but when Sarah went on to reaffirm her unshakable determination not to go through with the marriage, the maid's reaction was less encouraging.

"I don't blame you for feeling like that, miss, not one bit, but, you know, his lordship's right about one thing. Mistress will never let you cry off, nor will Mr. Peregrine. Fair cock-a-hoop they've been, both of 'em, ever since your engagement was announced."

"Yes, I know, and that is the most wretched part of the whole wretched business. How could they be so unfeeling? Perry, at least, must know what manner of man Lord Chayle is, and yet he gave his consent, and even told me how lucky I was to receive such an offer."

"Maybe Mr. Perry didn't set much store by it, miss," Lucy suggested. "Gentlemen don't, I'm told. It's the way of the Quality, and that's all there is to it. I dare say his lordship's no worse than a lot of others, and better than some."

"That does not excuse his conduct towards me," Sarah said adamantly. "Oh, Grandmama was right when she said he is deceitful and untrustworthy and arrogant! I should have paid more heed——!" She broke off, staring at Lucy. "Grandmama! Of course! She will take my part, I know."

"Likely she will, miss, but what good will that do? If her ladyship was in London it'd be a different matter, but she's in Kent, and you know she never travels in winter."

Sarah was staring at her, excitement growing in her eyes. "No, but what is to stop *me* travelling to *her*?"

"What's to stop——?" Lucy repeated blankly. "Miss Sarah, Clitterbury is all of fifty miles from here."

"Yes, we shall have to travel post. You must find out from the other servants the best place to hire a carriage, but be careful not to let them guess why you want to know. We can go out in the morning as though I were going to do some shopping—we can even get the footman to call up a hack for us and then give the driver fresh directions once we are out of sight of the house. We shall not be able to take much with us, only what you can hide under your cloak, but that does not matter. When we——!"

"Miss Sarah!" Lucy interrupted firmly. "Have you taken leave of your senses? You can't *run away*!"

A mutinous expression descended upon Sarah's

face. "Oh yes, I can, and what is more, I will! I will go to Grandmama and tell her how shamefully I have been treated and beg her to let me stay with her at Long Fallow Court. You know she has said, times without number, that she would like to have me to live with her."

"Miss, what would people say if you were to run off like that? Mistress would never forgive you for causing such a stir. No, and neither would his lordship!"

"But, Lucy, do you not see that that is precisely what I wish? He has refused to announce our engagement at an end, but this will give him such a disgust of me that he will be glad to do so." She paused, dwelling with relish upon the prospect of his lordship's discomfiture. "He said tonight that he did not intend to let me make him look a bigger fool than I have done already. Well, my lord, we shall see! We shall see just how foolish you can be made to look."

"Miss Sarah, don't do it!" Lucy pleaded. "Don't do something you'll regret all your life, just because you're in a temper. You'll ruin all your chances! Mistress will wash her hands of you, and what will be left for you then but to dance attendance on your grandma for the rest of her life? Stop a bit, miss, and think! That's all I ask."

Sarah paid no heed to this beyond an impatient shake of the head, and Lucy knew from past experience that her mistress had scarcely heard what she said. She waited with deep foreboding for Miss Lorymer's next remark.

"Matters really could not have fallen out more conveniently," Sarah said at length. "With Mama and Aunt Eliza confined to bed, it will be quite a long time before it occurs to anyone to wonder where we are, and since my Uncle Gundridge is out of town, and Perry and Charlie hunting in Leicestershire, there will be no one to come after us."

"There's his lordship," Lucy reminded her grimly.

"He will not follow, I give you my word, once he has read the letter I mean to write to him. This will make it plain, even to him, that nothing in the world can now persuade me to become his wife, and when it is known that I have run away rather than continue our engagement, he will look so intolerably foolish that he will wish never to see me again. Now, stop arguing, there's a dear soul, and go and find out where we must hire a carriage. I have to write that letter, and a note for Mama, and one for Lady Peterby telling her that her brother's scandalous conduct and heartless disregard for my feelings have led me to end our engagement. Oh, I am going to *enjoy* writing that, and the one to Chayle even more!"

"Miss Sarah," Lucy broke in sternly, "you listen to me! You know I'd do anything to help you, but stand by and watch you ruin your whole life I will not. Either you give up this crazy scheme, or I go straight to Mistress this minute and tell her what you mean to do. I mean it, I promise you!"

There was no doubt this time that Sarah was attending. She turned slowly from her writing desk, where she was already getting out pen and paper, and looked steadily at Lucy while half a minute ticked away. When at last she spoke, her voice sounded level and calm and not even the least bit annoyed.

"I cannot prevent you, Lucy, and I accept that you believe you would be acting for the best, but I will make you a promise, too. If you betray me to Mama, then the very next time I meet Mrs. Maitland in company, I shall tell her very clearly, and in the hearing of as many persons as possible, exactly what I think of her character, her manners, and her morals. Now what sort of a scandal do you suppose *that* would provoke?"

Lucy knew when to accept defeat, for she also knew that Sarah would carry out her threat to the letter, and even, while her anger lasted, revel in doing it. She chose the lesser of the two evils confronting her.

"All right, Miss Sarah," she said with a sigh, "you win. I'll go with you to Lady Marlby."

Chapter IV

Leaving the house with their real purpose unsus-
pected proved almost ridiculously easy. None of
the servants saw anything at all out of the way in
Miss Lorymer going shopping accompanied only by
her maid, since both her Mama and her aunt were
confined to bed; it was a bitterly cold day, with a
strong wind blowing icily from the northeast and
bringing with it occasional flurries of sleet, so there
was nothing remarkable in Lucy being huddled in a
voluminous hooded cloak, and no one guessed that
underneath it she was hugging a carpetbag contain-
ing a few necessities for her mistress and herself.
The driver of the hack summoned by the footman
accepted indifferently the change of destination,
and before long Sarah and Lucy found themselves
in the yard of a busy postinghouse.

For a young lady of quality, accompanied only
by a female servant, to be hiring her own postchaise,

was unusual, but with so many travellers constantly coming and going, this oddity was soon forgotten, and presently, with a sigh of relief, Sarah was able to relax against the cushions of the chaise, in the knowledge that the greatest obstacle had now been overcome. The changing of team and postboys at the various stages on the way to Kent would be simple by comparison.

She beguiled the first part of the journey by speculating, with relish, on the possible reaction of Justin Chayle to the letter which she had left to be delivered to his house. This had not been designed to spare his feelings or to minister to his self-esteem, and as a final gesture of defiance and repudiation she had enclosed in it the diamond ring, but she had not deigned to inform him of her destination. To her mother she had been less reticent on this point, but it was highly unlikely that Chayle would apply to Mrs. Lorymer for information. If her flight achieved its intended purpose, he would probably wish never to set eyes on any member of the Lorymer family again.

The weather, which had been reasonably bright when they set out from London, darkened as the day progressed, and by the time they left Rochester on the third stage of the journey the clouds were yellow-grey and threatening, hanging low over the bleak countryside. Within a few miles it had begun to snow heavily, the flakes spun by the wind into a whirling whiteness which blotted out all but the most immediate features of the landscape, and even penetrated, along with icy draughts, to the interior of the carriage through every chink of door and window. The two girls huddled together to find what warmth they could, but even so they felt chilled to the bone, and their hands and feet grew numb with cold.

The snow clung to the edges of the windows, building up thicker and thicker, so that in an alarmingly short space of time the whole panel of glass in the front of the chaise was obscured as though by a thick white curtain; of the side windows little more than peepholes remained, through which a glimmer of fading daylight filtered into the interior of the carriage. Their progress became slower and slower, and at last, cold and fright combined to wring a despairing exclamation from Lucy.

"Oh, Miss Sarah, we didn't ought to have come! We'll never get to her ladyship's house through this, and then what will become of us?"

"Nonsense, Lucy!" Pride compelled Sarah to reply with a show of confidence, although the abigail had merely put her own growing fears into words. "This is only a storm. I dare say it will be over directly."

Lucy leaned forward to peer through the remaining clear patch of the window beside her. "Don't you believe it, miss! It's almost dark, and not more than three o'clock, I'll warrant—and even if it does stop, like as not we're off the road already. Mark my words, we'll be lucky if we don't finish up in a ditch or a duck-pond and freeze to death."

"Pray do not be absurd!" Sarah said sharply. "It seems worse in here, because of the snow on the windows, but no doubt the postboy can perfectly well see the way. He knows the road, and is accustomed to travelling in all sorts of weather."

Abashed, Lucy relapsed into silence, and Sarah sat biting her lip and gripping her gloved hands very tightly together inside her muff. She could not really believe that the snow would stop. The weather, while she had still been able to see anything of it, had shown every sign of becoming steadily worse, and though she had rebuked Lucy's prophecies of disaster, she knew that it was by no means unknown for a vehicle in heavy snow to wander off the road or overturn in a drift. For the first time, doubts of the wisdom of her flight began to prick uneasily at Sarah's mind, mingled with resentment of the ill luck which, today of all days, had sent a blizzard sweeping across the county of Kent.

The chaise lurched along with agonising slowness, sometimes remaining stationary for several minutes while the tired horses heaved and strained, struggling to find sufficient purchase in the snow to drag the carriage a few yards further on its way. There seemed to be nothing left in all the world but the whirling whiteness, the screaming wind and the small, cold, almost lightless compartment in which she and Lucy huddled together, shivering with cold and apprehension. She was almost in despair when the assault of wind and snow suddenly lessened, and Lucy, pressing her face close to the nearly obliterated window, exclaimed with profound relief:

"Oh, miss, praise be, here's the inn at last! We're just pulling into the yard."

There was a pause, during which they heard the postboy shouting for an ostler; then he came to the door of the chaise and, after a brief struggle, succeeded in wrenching it open. Behind him, Sarah could make out a small, deserted stable yard and, to the left, just one lighted window breaking the dark, low-pitched bulk of the inn, dimly discernible through the swirling snow. She said in dismay:

"Surely this cannot be the posting house?"

"No, ma'am. The regular stage is a couple of miles along the road, but we dursn't try to go no further. There was times back yonder when I didn't think we was even going to get here."

"Where are we, then?"

"At the Rose in Hand, ma'am. It's a small house, but respectable, and Widow Ashlock, as keeps it, will look after you as snug as you please." Sarah hesitated, and he added with a touch of impatience: "Best step down, ma'am. The horses are spent, and I'm near froze to the marrow. We can't go on."

Sarah felt more than a little uneasy at the prospect of entering an unknown and obviously isolated inn, but she recognised the justice of the postboy's words, while the thought of warmth and hot food helped to overcome her misgivings. She allowed him to help her down, and with Lucy at her heels stumbled towards the house through snow which, even in the sheltered yard, was already more than ankle deep.

The door opened on to a narrow, stone-flagged passage, and as the two girls entered, a very stout, middle-aged woman in a neat gown and crisp white cap and apron emerged from the rear of the house.

"Mercy on us, ma'am, what a day to be travelling!" she exclaimed. "You must be chilled to the bone. Step into the coffee room, do! There's a good fire there."

She bustled forward to throw open a door, revealing the welcome sight of logs blazing in a fireplace the size of a small cave. Sarah, observing with relief that the room was unoccupied, and further reassured by Mrs. Ashlock's obvious respectability, went thankfully to seat herself in the inglenook, laying aside her muff and holding out her gloved hands to the blaze.

"Thank you," she said gratefully. "We should like some tea, if you please."

"I'll see to it at once, ma'am. For how many?"

"Just myself and my maid." Sarah felt the colour rise in her cheeks at Mrs. Ashlock's look of astonishment, but added composedly: "We should like a hot meal also, if that would be possible. As this is not a posting house we shall be obliged to rest the horses before going on to the regular stage."

Mrs. Ashlock stared. "Bless my soul, ma'am! You're never expecting to get any further tonight?"

"I must! It is most important." Sarah thought that the woman was looking at her now with a hint of suspicion, and added with dignity: "I am on my way to my grandmother's house—she is Lady Marlby of Long Fallow Court, near Clitterbury—and the matter is urgent."

"But, ma'am, Clitterbury's all of twelve miles

from here, and 'twill be black dark in an hour.
You'll never get your postboy to turn out again in
weather like this."

"But I must go on!" There was a tremor now in
Sarah's voice in spite of all her efforts to keep it
steady. "I must reach Long Fallow."

"That's as may be, ma'am, begging your pardon,
but you'll not be able to do it before morning, if
then."

Mrs. Ashlock spoke with a touch of asperity, for
she was beginning to think that there was something
decidedly odd about this fashionably dressed young
lady who travelled in a hired post chaise with only
an equally youthful abigail for company. The Rose
in Hand might not cater much for the Quality, but
she knew that its daughters usually travelled in their
own carriages, and very seldom without some male
relative or thoroughly dependable manservant to
look after them, so it was unthinkable that one of
them would have been permitted to set out unes-
corted in such weather as this.

"In some sort of scrape, I'll be bound," Mrs.
Ashlock thought shrewdly. "I wonder if Lady Marlby really is her grandma? Her ladyship's got married daughters, so it could be true—though from
what I've heard she's a real tartar, and not the sort a
young maid in trouble would turn to for help. Still,
true or not, she'll never get to Long Fallow tonight."

"Now, miss, you listen to me," she said after a
moment, less sharply but with the kind of firmness
she would have used to her own daughter had that
stolid maiden been bent on folly. "Even if you

could persuade your postboy to set out, which you won't, and even if you got as far as the posting house, which would be a miracle, you certainly wouldn't get any further. By morning your horses will be rested, and in daylight there's a chance you could get through to Clitterbury, but I'd be going against my duty as a Christian if I let you set off now, because like as not you'd catch your death."

Lucy, standing beside her mistress and in the heartiest agreement with every word Mrs. Ashlock had uttered, said urgently: "Oh, miss, do let's put up here! I know it might not be quite the thing for you to stay at an inn with only me here, but what else can you do on such a night? Besides, who's to know?"

Sarah grasped her arm and pulled her down so that Lucy's head was close to her own. "It is not that, you stupid girl!" she said in a fierce whisper. "I have not enough money to put up anywhere. As it was, I was depending upon Grandmama to pay for the last stage."

Lucy straightened up, staring at her with such transparent dismay that Mrs. Ashlock's suspicions were instantly aroused. She had not been able to hear what Sarah said, but that it was unwelcome to the abigail was clear enough.

This was equally clear to another and as yet unobserved witness. While they talked, a door on the far side of the room had opened quietly, and the young man who was the sole occupant of the parlour to which it led had been standing on the threshold, silently observing them. His gaze travelled

speculatively over Sarah's demure yet fashionable
attire, noted the anxiety in the youthful face framed
by the velvet-trimmed bonnet, and the uneasiness
and then the blank dismay of the young maidser-
vant, and took in also the gathering frown on Mrs.
Ashlock's brow. Obviously the lady was in difficulties, and needed a knight errant, and what had
threatened to be an exceedingly boring sojourn at
the Rose in Hand might well prove to be quite the
reverse.

"You know, ma'am," he remarked conversationally, "Mrs. Ashlock tells you no more than the
truth. I came from the direction of Clitterbury earlier this afternoon, and even then the roads were in
shocking state. By now, they are bound to be impassable."

Sarah gasped and swung round. The speaker was
a slim, dark-haired young man of medium height,
good-looking in a rather obvious way, and dressed
in a style which suggested aspirations to dandyism.
Meeting her glance, he came farther into the room
and bowed.

"I beg your pardon, ma'am. I fear I startled you.
The truth is that I was so much astonished to hear
the sound of other guests arriving in such weather
as this that sheer curiosity prompted me to look into
this room." He glanced inquiringly at Lucy and
then at Mrs. Ashlock. "I apprehend that you are
travelling alone? In the circumstances, an uncomfortable situation for a lady, so allow *me* to offer
you any assistance which may lie with my power.

My name is John Roman, and I am entirely at your service."

The dismay which Sarah had felt at his first appearance was in no way soothed by this smooth speech. She had been toying with the idea of confiding her financial difficulties to Mrs. Ashlock, for the landlady seemed a kind and motherly person, and since Clitterbury was only twelve miles away, Lady Marlby's name must be known to her and might persuade her to extend credit. The arrival on the scene of Mr. Roman altered everything. It would be one thing to spend the night, with only Lucy as chaperone, as Mrs. Ashlock's sole guest; to do so when the only other person putting up at the inn was a young gentleman would be enough to ruin her reputation if it ever became known. She looked pleadingly at Mrs. Ashlock.

"Is there truly no way of reaching Clitterbury tonight? It is so very important."

The widow's lips tightened impatiently. "No, miss, there's not! You'll be lucky if you can go on tomorrow. It wouldn't be the first time we've been snowed up for days."

"Believe me, ma'am," John Roman added persuasively, "there is no alternative to putting up here. I have already bespoken the private parlour. There is an excellent fire there, and it is a smaller and more cosy room than this, so why not join me there and let Mrs. Ashlock bring you something hot to drink? Then we may be comfortable."

She cast him a look of astonished indignation, but this was met by a stare of such bold appraisal

that the colour rushed into her cheeks, and she was
seized by the conviction that he was somehow aware
of her financial dilemma and determined to take
full advantage of it. Even Mrs. Ashlock, who a few
moments ago had seemed kind and motherly, now
appeared, to Sarah's overwrought imagination, to
have become suspicious and hostile.

Suddenly, as well as being tired and cold and
hungry, Sarah was frightened, too. She had been so
sure that she could fend for herself, but she had
never envisaged a plight such as this. If she paid for
a night's lodging for herself and Lucy, she would
not have enough money to settle with the postboy
who had brought them here, which in turn would
make it impossible to engage one of his colleagues
to take them the rest of the way; and suppose Mrs.
Ashlock were right, and the snow trapped them
here for several days? She did not know what to do;
panic made it impossible for her to think clearly,
and her strongest inclination was to burst into tears.

A sudden draught of icy air swept into the room
as the outer door opened, then closed again with a
slam. A firm, unhurried footstep sounded in the
passage, and as the occupants of the coffee room
looked instinctively towards the source of these
sounds, a tall gentleman in a many-caped, snow-
whitened greatcoat appeared in the doorway. He
paused there, surveying the scene before him from
beneath haughtily lifted brows. Lucy uttered a gasp
of astonishment and alarm, and Sarah sat as though
turned to stone, staring across the room into the
hard grey eyes of Justin Chayle.

Chapter V

In the instant of recognition, her first reaction was sheer relief. This feeling was followed in rapid succession by alarm, dismay, and resentment, but it could not be entirely obliterated even though he was looking at her with eyes as wintry as the weather. However angry he might be, and in spite of the humiliation his arrival must bring, at least she was not now alone among strangers.

That brief survey of the room, and of the varied expressions on the faces of its occupants, had enabled Justin to form a tolerably accurate estimate of the situation. He strolled forward, removing his hat and saying pleasantly to Sarah:

"So there you are, my dear! I knew I could not be far behind you. It was most imprudent, you know, to set out from London in that headlong fashion, for I am sure your grandmother's illness is nowhere near as serious as you imagine."

Sarah continued to stare at him, still too bemused to follow the lead he had given her. A flicker of impatience showed for a moment in his eyes, but before the pause had lasted long enough for her lack of response to be remarked, he had turned to Mrs. Ashlock.

"I am Lord Chayle. It is clearly impossible for Miss Lorymer and me to continue our journey, so I shall require your best bedchamber for her and her maid, another for myself, and a private parlour. And quarters for my groom." He saw that the good lady was now looking more suspicious than ever, and added with a smile: "I should perhaps explain to you, ma'am, that Miss Lorymer and I are engaged to be married, and at present on our way to the home of her grandmother, Lady Marlby."

Mrs. Ashlock's brow cleared as if by magic, no doubt due as much, Sarah thought resentfully, to the charm of his lordship's smile as to his explanation. Mr. Roman, who had been eyeing Justin with marked antagonism, looked disconcerted.

"Well, my lord, I'll be happy to oblige you as best I can," Mrs. Ashlock said doubtfully, "but my best bedchamber's already bespoke by this gentleman, and the parlour, too, though he *was* saying, just before your lordship came in, that miss could have the use of that if she chose."

"The bedchamber, too, of course," Roman put in hurriedly. "Pray have my gear moved out of it, Mrs. Ashlock. I shall be quite comfortable in one of your smaller rooms."

"Exceedingly civil of you, sir," Justin said with cool courtesy. "Pray accept my thanks."

"I am happy to be of service, my lord," the other assured him, bowing. "Permit me to present myself. My name is John Roman, and I, too, have been stranded here by the weather."

Justin favoured him with a cool, measuring glance and bowed slightly in response. Then, turning to Sarah, he took her hand and said in the same pleasant tone: "Let us avail ourselves of Mr. Roman's generosity, ma'am, and go into the parlour. It is not fitting for you to sit in a public room."

Sarah, not relishing the prospect of a tête-à-tête with his lordship, was tempted to protest, but the compelling grasp on her hand, and the look in the unsmiling grey eyes, warned her that to do so would be useless and would end in humiliating defeat. She therefore allowed him to help her up, and preceded him into the parlour. Lucy, torn between fear of Lord Chayle and reluctance to desert her mistress, hesitated in miserable uncertainty until an imperious gesture signalled her to accompany them.

Justin paused long enough to address the landlady. "We will dine as soon as it can conveniently be arranged, and meanwhile, pray be good enough to bring a bowl of hot rum punch to the parlour."

The door closed behind him. Mrs. Ashlock hurried away, and John Roman, a faint frown creasing his brow, threw himself down in the seat vacated by Sarah, and sat there staring into the fire in a brooding fashion. The wind roared and howled in the wide, old-fashioned chimney, and drove the snow to pile thicker and thicker against the latticed windows.

Inside the parlour, Sarah had gone to stand by the fire, pulling off her gloves and jerking them nervously between her hands. Justin watched her for a moment or two and then turned to Lucy, waiting apprehensively just inside the door.

"You heard what I said just now to the landlady?"

"Yes, my lord."

"Then be sure that you remember it. This morning Mrs. Lorymer received a letter informing her that Lady Marlby is ill and wishes to see her. Because Mrs. Lorymer is confined to her bed with a severe cold, and neither of the young gentlemen is in town, your mistress, mistakenly supposing that I, too, was out of town, rashly set off alone to go to her grandmother. I was informed of this by Mrs. Lorymer, and immediately followed. That is what you are to say if anyone questions you. That, and no more. You understand?"

"Yes, my lord," Lucy faltered again.

"Very well. You may go." Lucy hesitated, looking anxiously from him to Sarah, and he added sardonically: "You need not scruple to leave Miss Lorymer alone with me. She stands in no need of your protection."

Lucy, flushing scarlet, cast an apologetic glance at Sarah, dropped a curtsy and thankfully made her escape. In nerve-wracking silence, Chayle put down his hat and gloves, took off his greatcoat and threw it across a chair, then strolled unhurriedly forward to join Sarah by the fire.

"Your abigail looks at me as though she expected me to beat you," he remarked, "and if I were to fulfill her expectations it would be no more than you deserve. You were determined, were you not, to set the world by the ears?"

Sarah took a deep breath, willing her voice not to tremble. "I was concerned, sir, only to convince you that I meant what I said last night. Our engagement is at an end."

To her intense chagrin, he let the statement pass as though it had not been uttered. "Your concern, ma'am, as we both very well know, was to demonstrate to me that I was mistaken when I said that you had no choice but to obey me. Also to place me in as awkward a situation as you could devise, though you cannot seriously have supposed that I would make a fool of myself by attending my sister's party without you."

She looked defiantly up at him. "I explained everything to Lady Peterby in the note I sent, making her my apologies."

"I am aware of that. As it happens, however, Georgiana has sufficient affection for me to keep the information to herself, and to lend me every assistance in preventing your wilfulness from becoming known. The story which I outlined to your abigail will also be offered tonight in explanation of our absence, and only your mother and your aunt, and Mrs. Blackstead, will know that it is not true. There may be a little speculation, but it will not last."

His calm assurance nettled her beyond endurance. "Perhaps not, but how does your lordship propose to prevent me from informing our acquaintance, once I return to London, that our marriage will not now take place?"

He did not reply at once, and she felt the first stirring of triumph as she watched him take out his snuffbox, open it with an expert flick of the thumb, and thoughtfully inhale a pinch. Then he closed the box with a snap and looked at her, faintly smiling.

"I could not prevent it, of course, but do you really wish to appear so intolerably foolish? Your family would deny it, and so would I. Moreover, the opportunity to make such a declaration is not likely to be offered to you. I should perhaps tell you that I am the bearer of a message from your Mama. Either you will undertake to behave yourself, or I am to convey you straight home to Hampshire and leave you there in the care of your sisters' governess."

"I do not believe it," she said angrily. "You cannot possibly have spoken to Mama. She is ill in bed."

"True, but though she is extremely unwell, she got up in order to receive me, so that we might determine how best to deal with this escapade of yours. Let us hope that she will suffer no ill effects from being obliged to leave her bed."

Sarah looked conscience-stricken. "Oh, she should not have done so! I did not think—"

"Precisely! You did not think of anything but your own wounded vanity. You supposed that with your brothers and Mr. Gundridge absent from London, and Mrs. Lorymer and her sister confined to their beds, you could embark upon this ill-judged venture with no fear of pursuit. You are a poor judge of character, ma'am, or you would not have left *me* out of your calculations."

"It certainly did not occur to me that you would trouble yourself to come after me. That was, indeed, an error of judgment."

He looked at her with an expression she could not quite define. "Did it not occur to you, either, that when I learned of your rashness I might feel a considerable degree of concern?"

"Since you have shown so little regard for me, sir," she retorted, "I must confess that it did not. I knew that you would be exceedingly angry, and, frankly, I was glad of it."

In this assumption she was quite correct, for Justin was very angry indeed. He had been furious with her the night before, and his temper had only partially cooled when it was fanned to white heat again by the return of her engagement ring, and by the tone of the letter which accompanied it. Mingled with his anger, however, had been a certain anxiety over the various mischances which might befall her on her journey, and which presently were graphically, if unnecessarily, enumerated to him by a distraught Mrs. Lorymer. During the past hour or two, while he struggled in pursuit of his errant bride through freezing cold and blinding snow, anxiety had grown until it conquered anger completely, and it had been an immense relief to find her safe at the

Rose in Hand. Unfortunately, this more charitable frame of mind had not survived more than a few minutes' conversation with her.

"I *am* exceedingly angry," he said with a snap, "though whether or not you will continue to be glad of it, Miss Lorymer, remains to be seen. You choose to attribute to me none but the basest motives, and if that attitude is designed to convince me that we should not marry, let me tell you that you are very much out in your reckoning. If, on the other hand, you truly believe me to be of so reprehensible a character, I am astonished that you ever consented to become my wife."

"At that time, sir," she replied with dignity, "I was unacquainted with your true character. Now that I *am* aware of it, nothing can prevail upon me to marry you."

"No?" he said ironically. "Yet I have already indicated to you that your family has every intention that you shall."

"Not *all* my family, sir. Oh, if only I could have reached Grandmama's house!"

"I am at a loss to understand," Justin remarked, "just what you suppose Lady Marlby can do. Oh, I am aware that she and my mother were at dagger-drawing for years, and that she looks with disfavour upon our engagement, but her opinion carries no weight, you know. Your brother Peregrine is your legal guardian."

Sarah regarded him resentfully. Although she was well aware of these facts, she had chosen to ignore them, but now, presented in Chayle's calm, ironical voice, they could be ignored no longer. Of course Grandmama could do nothing; she would sympathise, and express her opinion forcibly to Perry and to Mama, but in the face of all the worldly advantages which Chayle could offer, her protests would fall upon deaf ears. Sarah knew it, and so, infuriatingly, did Chayle himself.

"One is therefore forced to the conclusion," he went on, "that today's escapade is merely a gesture of defiance, a means of inflicting the punishment you appear to feel I deserve. I trust it has relieved your feelings, for I can assure you that it has achieved nothing else."

She was spared the necessity of making any reply by Mrs. Ashlock, who came in bearing a steaming bowl of punch on a tray. Setting this down on the table, she said to Justin:

"I've brought two glasses, my lord, as I thought the young lady might be glad of a little, just to warm her. She must be mortal cold still."

"An excellent notion," he agreed pleasantly. "Please see that the abigail has something warming also, and furnish my groom with whatever he desires."

Sarah, still standing stiffly by the fire, made a push for independence. "I would much prefer a cup of tea. In fact, I had already bespoken it when you arrived."

"You shall have tea later, my child," Justin said calmly, shaking his head in answer to Mrs. Ashlock's inquiring look. "In the usual manner, after we have dined. At present, a glass of punch will do you far more good."

Smiling indulgently, Mrs. Ashlock withdrew. Justin ladled punch into both glasses and offered one to Sarah; she shook her head.

"No, thank you, my lord," she said primly, "Mama would not approve."

"Mama need never know. Come, drink it! It will ward off any chill, and who knows? It may even put you in a better humour."

She cast him a look of dislike but took the glass, for she felt in real need of something hot to drink and it was plain that, thanks to his lordship's high-handedness, she was not going to get any tea. She sipped the punch cautiously, choked a little over the spirit in it, but was pleasantly surprised by its sweetness and the tang of lemon juice.

There was a high-backed wooden armchair with crimson cushions on either side of the fireplace. Justin pulled one of them closer to the blaze and held out an imperious hand.

"Come, sit down and take off your bonnet. We are snowbound here for the night, and possibly for several days, and this pose of persecuted innocence will be as wearing for you to maintain as for me to endure. Almost as wearing as to spend the whole time quarrelling, so let us cry quits, and see if we cannot contrive a little better from now on."

After a little hesitation she complied with the first part of this suggestion, for she recognised the com-

mon sense of what he said. Laying aside the bonnet
with a sigh of relief, she patted her soft dark curls
into place, unbuttoned her pelisse, and sat down,
stretching her toes towards the warmth of the fire.
She drank a little more of the punch, and felt a
pleasant glow creeping through her veins.

Justin had emptied his glass and gone to the table
to refill it. Then he thought of something else and
turned back to the fire, taking Sarah's ring from his
pocket.

"Put this on. Since I have informed the landlady
that we are betrothed, it will be as well if you are
seen to be wearing my ring."

Sarah put down her glass rather hurriedly and
thrust her left hand behind her. "No! I will try not
to quarrel with you while we are in this awkward
situation, but that does not mean that anything has
changed."

"Precisely! Nothing has changed, and we are still
engaged." He grasped her arm, drew the hand gently but firmly from behind her, compelled her to un-
clench it, and slid the ring on to her finger. Still
gripping her hand between his own, he went on:
"Endeavour to reconcile yourself to the thought, for
I intend to waste no more time arguing over it. Now
are you going to listen to what I have to say, or must
I continue to hold you in this very overbearing fashion?"

"I will listen," she said breathlessly, hoping that
he was unaware of the treacherous pounding of her
heart. As he let her go and moved to seat himself in

the other armchair, she added provocatively: "I have no choice, have I, situated as I am?"

"None whatsoever," he agreed calmly. "I hold you at a most unfair disadvantage, but allow me to point out that it is entirely your own fault. Your behaviour at Lady Bellingham's was outrageous, and today's prank even worse, but had I been aware of the provocation you had suffered, I might have been less severe in my comments. It was only this morning I learned the truth of that." He saw that she found this hard to believe, and added in explanation: "As you know, my sister Georgiana was also present at Lady Bellingham's. A remark she overheard after we left aroused her suspicions, and a short conversation with Mrs. Blackstead put her in possession of the facts." He paused, then added dryly: "Her sympathy, I may say, is with you."

"Then it is more than I deserve," she replied with a candour that surprised him, "for I have put her in a shockingly awkward situation by depriving her party of its two principal guests. It would not be wonderful if she never spoke to me again."

"You need have no fear of that, but it is not of Georgiana that I wish to speak to you at present. It is of Mrs. Maitland." She flashed him a startled, incredulous glance, and he added with a slight smile: "Yes, I know that last night I rebuked *you* severely for doing so, but it is plain that if we are ever to reach an understanding, matters cannot be left thus between us."

He was silent for a moment, looking frowningly

into the fire, and then he raised his eyes again to
meet her doubtful, slightly suspicious gaze. Holding
it compellingly with his own level regard, he said
quietly:

"My association with Mrs. Maitland ended before you consented to become my wife, and I have
no intention of begging your pardon for something
which concerned you not at all. For the embarrassment which you were made to suffer as a direct result of it, however, I do ask your forgiveness. You
were placed in an intolerable situation, and the
fault was very largely mine."

The last thing Sarah had expected from him was
any kind of apology, and for several seconds she
could only stare at him in astonished silence. At
length she said, stammering a little:

"I was at fault, too, for, provocation or no, I
should not have given Mrs. Maitland the cut direct.
It—it was undignified! Only she was being so hateful, in that odiously kind way, telling me how pretty
I looked, and what a charming gown, and all the
time laughing in her sleeve because I am plain, and
Mama *will* make me wear these insipid colours.
Coming so soon after the horrid things she had said
earlier it was the last straw, and I lost my temper."

"It would have been surprising if you had not,"
he agreed calmly. "Tell me, why do you think so
poorly of your own looks?"

Her gaze lifted quickly to meet his, the big brown
eyes wide and distrustful, as though she suspected
him of mockery. "Because I *am* plain. So dark, and

such a little dab of a creature. All my sisters are tall and beautiful, and Amy, the next youngest, is quite dazzling."

"And you, my poor child, have always been made to feel the ugly duckling among this flight of swans?" he said with a perception that astonished her. "But you are wrong, you know. Your looks are not quite in the common way, and you do not appear to advantage in the clothes chosen for you, but no one with any pretension to good taste could regard you as plain."

"It is kind of you to say so, my lord," she replied, still eyeing him dubiously, "but they do, you know. At home in Hampshire I am commonly referred to as 'the plain Miss Lorymer,' and oh! I cannot tell you how much I hate it."

Even as she spoke, she was conscious of amazement at being able to confide in him, to confess to feelings which she had always been at pains to conceal. Even an hour ago she could not have envisaged such a thing, but in the past few minutes he had become approachable to a degree she had hitherto only dreamed of, and suddenly she was no longer in awe of him. Oddly enough, it seemed that their quarrel, and the angry, biting things they had said to each other, had somehow brought them closer together.

"You would be a very odd sort of female indeed if you did *not* hate it," he agreed gravely, though now there was a glimmer of amusement deep down in his eyes. "However, if you insist upon being guided by the opinions of others, let me assure you that I would not have asked you to be my wife had I not found your person as pleasing as your manners."

Colour rushed up into her cheeks, but she could not resist saying: "I thank your lordship for the compliment, but you have now discovered, have you not, that my manners are not at all what you supposed?"

"I admit that you have surprised me. If, twenty-four hours ago, someone had told me that you are capable of the kind of escapade which has placed us in our present situation, I should have supposed him to be deranged."

"I lost my temper, you see," she said apologetically. "First with Mrs. Maitland, and then with you. It is only when I am very angry that I do these outrageous things."

His lips twitched. "Do you lose your temper very often, Miss Lorymer?"

"Oh no, indeed! You must not think me one of those tiresome women who are forever flying into a miff. In the general way I am quite even-tempered."

"I am relieved to hear it!" His amusement was quite open now, but it was kindly, as though he were laughing with her, and not at her. "If it were otherwise, I fear ours would be an unquiet household, since my own temper, as you have learned by now, is not as equable as one might wish."

She was given no opportunity to reply to this, for a tap on the door heralded the entry into the room of an apple-cheeked young woman, a younger but scarcely less stout edition of Mrs. Ashlock, who bobbed a curtsy and announced, in the breathless monotone of one repeating a lesson learned by heart:

"If you please, my lord, Mother says dinner can be served in an hour, and if miss wants to go up to her bedchamber it's all ready, and her portmanteau carried there, and her abigail waiting. And I'm to show her the way." She paused, beamed a triumphant smile, and then added belatedly: "When it pleases her."

"Thank you. You may wait outside, and Miss Lorymer will come directly."

Miss Ashlock dropped another curtsy, and withdrew. Sarah said in complete bewilderment:

"But I have no portmanteau. I was able to bring only the barest necessities, which Lucy smuggled out under her cloak."

"So we supposed," he said with a smile. "The portmanteau came with me. Your mother packed it herself, so you will find it, I am sure, to contain everything you may need."

"Mama should not have put herself to so much trouble, unwell as she is," Sarah said contritely. "Oh dear, what a deal of bother I have caused her! And you, too, my lord, causing you to be stranded here at this lonely little inn, which I am sure is not at all what you have been used to, and which you must find excessively dull and disagreeable."

"Not at all," he countered politely. "I am coming rapidly to the conclusion, Miss Lorymer, that dullness is one thing which I am never likely to suffer in your company." He saw the distrustful expression in her eyes again, and laughed. "Seriously, though, do you not agree that our present situation offers us a unique opportunity to become better acquainted? We do not yet know each other very well, and that, I feel, is something which should be remedied."

Though Sarah could think of nothing she would like more than to become better acquainted with his lordship, she did not know what reply to make to this. To dissemble her confusion she got up out of her chair, saying rather breathlessly:

"No doubt you are right, sir. Now I think I will go upstairs, for I feel shockingly untidy after that dreadful journey."

He had risen also. "By all means, and I trust you will find your room tolerably comfortable. We shall meet again at dinner."

He went to open the door for her, and Miss Ashlock, who had been hovering anxiously outside, promptly dropped another curtsy and, respectfully desiring Miss Lorymer to follow her, backed away across the coffee room as though in the presence of royalty, a courtesy which placed a considerable strain upon Sarah's gravity. She was suddenly feeling extraordinarily lighthearted.

Chapter VI

The best bedchamber at the Rose in Hand was old-fashioned and comfortable, dominated by a huge fourposter. In the whitewashed walls, great supporting beams showed black with age, the window was long and low and the worn, uneven floorboards polished to a perilous degree of slipperiness. Both bed and window were curtained with crimson stuff, and as a bright fire burned in the grate, its glow mingling with the light of several candles, the effect was one of extreme cosiness, emphasised by the howling of the blizzard about the house. Sarah, entering, remarked on this fact with spontaneous sincerity, and Miss Ashlock went away beaming more widely than ever with gratification.

"It *is* a comfortable room, miss, and no mistake," Lucy remarked, relieving her mistress of bonnet, muff, and gloves, and laying these aside to help her

off with her pelisse. "A deal more comfortable, I'll
be bound, than you would have had if his lordship
hadn't come along, so it's well he did come, for all I
nearly dropped with fright when I saw him. Oh,
Miss Sarah, is he very angry?"

"He was," Sarah admitted, moving closer to the
fire. "He gave me a most tremendous scold, but as
we may be stranded here for several days, he says
we should not spend the whole time quarrelling but
use it instead to become better acquainted."

"A good thing, too," Lucy said bluntly. "I know
it's the way of the Quality, Miss Sarah, and not
for the likes of me to question, but I tell you to
your face, it seems downright wicked to me to expect any girl to marry a man she's met no more than
half a dozen times at parties and suchlike, and
never even spoken to without someone standing by.
If it means you and his lordship coming to better
terms with each other, I hope we may be snowed up
here for a week."

"Good gracious, Lucy, I hope not! Lord Chayle
would be distracted with boredom, and glad to
quarrel with me just to relieve the tedium. But I
dare say we shall be able to go on our way in the
morning."

"Don't you believe it, Miss Sarah," Lucy replied,
turning from the cupboard where she had been putting away Sarah's outdoor clothes. "Polly Ashlock
was telling me they've often been cut off for days
after a storm like this, so they always keep the house
well provisioned in winter. We shan't go hungry, at

any rate! What a mercy his lordship brought your portmanteau. Will you be changing your dress before you go down?"

"Oh yes, I think so, for this one is sadly crumpled. I see you have the embroidered cambric there. I will wear that, and the Norwich shawl."

Lucy laid the chosen garments on the bed, and busied herself with helping her mistress to change. When Sarah was ready, she suggested that she ought to accompany her as far as the parlour door. Sarah stared at her in astonishment.

"In heaven's name, Lucy, why? I have only to go along the passage, down the stairs and through the coffee room, and it is not as though this were a large and busy posting house. There is hardly anyone else here."

"There's that Mr. Roman," Lucy said darkly. "He's been asking all sorts of impudent questions about you and his lordship, and I didn't like the way he behaved when we first saw him."

"Neither did I, but though he might have been tempted *then* to undue familiarity, he will scarcely try to go beyond what is proper now that he knows me to be under the protection of my future husband."

"Oh, his lordship would soon send him about his business, I'll be bound," Lucy agreed with relish. "You go down alone then, miss, if you must, and if Mr. Roman's below, you pay no heed to him."

John Roman was in the coffee room, but no fault could have been found with his manner. He jumped up as soon as Sarah entered and went to open the parlour door for her; she inclined her head with a smile of thanks as she went past him, but she had scarcely set foot in the smaller room when she was arrested by the sound of a mild commotion from the direction of the stable yard and the door leading to it. She paused and half turned, and she and Mr. Roman exchanged a startled, disbelieving glance, for, incredible as it seemed with the blizzard still raging with unabated fury, it appeared that a number of people were arriving at the inn. Men's voices could be heard, in astonished question and urgent answer, and then Mrs. Ashlock's brisk tones. Mr. Roman started towards the door, but before he reached it, it was flung open and Polly Ashlock burst in.

"Oh, miss, such a to-do!" she exclaimed. "It's the passengers off the London stage. The coach be in the ditch half a mile back, and they've had to make their way here as best they could. And a lady among 'em, poor soul! Swooned away, she did, as soon as she set foot in the house, and no wonder."

Even as she spoke, she was followed into the room by a burly young man, obviously her brother, who bore a limp female figure in his arms. Sarah saw a blue velvet pelisse, wet with melting snow, and a fashionable bonnet falling back from guinea-gold curls and a white, exhausted face; she uttered an exclamation of concern and moved forward a few paces, saying pityingly:

"Oh, poor creature! Bring her through to the parlour, where it is more private."

He hesitated, but was urged forward again by a

brisk poke in the back from his mother, who had
followed him into the room.

"Get on with you, Joe, and do as miss says!
Carry the poor young woman to that chair by the
fire."

He did as he was told, beating a hasty retreat as
soon as he had set down his burden. Mrs. Ashlock,
commanding him to look after the other passengers
from the stagecoach, and Polly to bring a glass of
brandy at once, shut the door on them and hurried
to join Sarah, who had produced smelling salts from
her reticule and was trying to restore the unknown
to her senses.

"That's right, miss," the widow commended her.
"We'll soon have her round, poor thing." She un-
tied the strings of the bonnet and cast it aside, loos-
ened the pelisse, which was buttoned tightly to the
throat, and then pulled off the girl's gloves in order
to chafe her hands. "Mercy on us, her skirts are
soaked clean through! She ought to be got straight
to bed, though where I'm to put her is more than I
can tell, for we're not used to having so many people putting up here, and that's a fact!"

"She can share my room," Sarah said impulsive-
ly. "There is the trestle-bed for Lucy, and it would
be quite wicked of me to keep that huge fourposter
all to myself when this poor girl is in such a fix, and
you are so pressed for space."

Mrs. Ashlock looked doubtful. "Well, miss, I
don't know, I'm sure! It would be a load off my
mind, I'll own, but it might not be fitting, her being

a stranger to you, and travelling by the common
stage. What would his lordship say?"

"He would say, as I do, that in such circumstances we must all do what we can to help one another," Sarah declared, recklessly committing
Chayle to a point of view she was by no means sure
he would hold. "Besides, she has the appearance of
a lady, even though she was on the stagecoach."

Mrs. Ashlock's misgivings were not wholly
soothed, but she was at her wits' end to know how
to accommodate all the unexpected guests thrust
upon her by the storm. Most of her attention had
been given to the woman, but she had observed that
there were four or five male passengers from the
stagecoach, as well as the coachman and the guard.
Beds of some sort would have to be found for all of
them, and with the "Quality" already occupying the
three best bedchambers, the limited resources of the
Rose in Hand would be stretched to the uttermost.
If the two young women and the abigail could share
Miss Lorymer's room, the most pressing problem of
accommodation would be solved with complete propriety.

"It's very obliging of you, miss," she said gratefully, "and if you're sure his lordship won't object,
I'll do as you say. As soon as Polly brings that brandy, I'll send her up to put a warming pan to the
sheets."

At this point the young woman across whose unconscious form the discussion was taking place
stirred in the chair and murmured something unin-

telligible. Then she opened bewildered blue eyes and looked in a dazed fashion from one to the other of the two faces bending above her.

"That's better," Mrs. Ashlock said in a heartening tone. "Don't you fret, my dear, for all's well now." She straightened up as she spoke, adding in a vexed tone: "Where's Polly got to with that brandy? Hanging about the menfolk, I'll be bound, instead of doing as I told her."

She bustled across to the door; the girl in blue, who had begun to shiver violently, said through chattering teeth: "I remember now. The stagecoach overturned, and we had to get out into the snow. It was so cold . . ." She looked up sharply to meet Sarah's sympathetic gaze. "What place is this?"

"It is an inn called the Rose in Hand."

For a second or two the young woman continued to regard her, then she raised an unsteady hand to her eyes, partially hiding her face. Sarah, remembering her own misgivings at finding herself stranded, unprotected, at a strange inn, went on reassuringly:

"There are several travellers stranded here by the storm, and the inn is very crowded in consequence, so I hope you will not object to sharing a room with me and my maid. It is the only practical arrangement."

The other woman made no response to this. Mrs. Ashlock returned with a glass of brandy which she urged her to drink, and the girl obeyed in silence, still shivering so violently that the glass rattled against her teeth. Steam had begun to rise gently from her skirts, sodden to the knee with melting snow.

"You *must* get out of those wet clothes," Sarah said anxiously. "Mrs. Ashlock, if you will send Lucy to me, we will look after this lady, for I am sure you have a great many other things to arrange."

"I would be grateful, miss," Mrs. Ashlock admitted, "for if I don't get back to the kitchen soon the dinner will spoil. I've sent Polly up with the warming pan, so the lady can get to bed as soon as she feels able."

She hurried away; after a pause, the girl in blue said rather grudgingly: "You are very kind. I'm sorry to put you to so much trouble."

"Nonsense!" Sarah replied with a smile. "It would be a sorry thing indeed if I could not offer assistance to someone in so uncomfortable a fix. *I* was fortunate enough to reach the inn in my carriage, but I can imagine how disagreeable and frightening it must have been to be obliged to go on foot."

"The coachman did offer to put me up on one of the horses," her companion admitted, "but I'm scared of the brutes at the best of times, let alone in the middle of a blizzard, and I preferred to walk. The other passengers helped me, but I was obliged to leave all my baggage in the coach."

"Oh, pray do not put yourself about on that account! I can lend you what you will need for tonight, and my maid will attend to the clothes you are wearing now. No doubt it will be possible to recover your property once the storm is over."

"Yes, but it will probably all be ruined by damp by that time." She seemed to realise that this sounded ungracious, and added defensively: "I beg your pardon. You will think me a fool to be fretting over such a thing when I should be thankful just to be somewhere safe and warm, but almost everything I own is in that stagecoach."

"Indeed I do not! I should be just as distressed in your circumstances, and can understand your feelings very well." Sarah paused, looking searchingly at her companion. "Forgive me, but have we not met before? I am Sarah Lorymer."

"No, we've not met," the other woman replied decisively, adding, after a perceptible pause: "My name is Frensham. Chloe Frensham."

Sarah, frowning a little, murmured a polite acknowledgment. She was puzzled, for she could not rid herself of the feeling that Miss Frensham's face, to which a trace of colour was now returning, was vaguely familiar. She was strikingly good-looking, even though somewhat older than Sarah had at first thought, probably twenty-five or so. Her golden hair was dressed in the latest mode, and her clothes, even in their present bedraggled condition, showed a rather dashing elegance. Appearance, speech, and manner suggested a person of gentility, yet there was some subtle quality—a greater self-assurance, perhaps, than was usual, or even a trace of hardness —which struck a faintly discordant note. Sarah had taken her for a young matron, but she now saw that she wore no wedding ring.

"Did I understand you to say, ma'am," Miss

Frensham asked suddenly, "that a number of travellers are stranded here tonight?"

"Indeed you did. Apart from myself and my maid, and the gentleman to whom I am betrothed, who is escorting me on my journey, there is another gentleman who was here when we arrived, and now, of course, everyone from the stagecoach." Mention of Chayle thrust a sudden, probing finger of uneasiness into her mind as she wondered again how he would react to the arrangements she had made for Miss Frensham, and she added diffidently: "Do you yet feel strong enough to go upstairs? The thing is that my betrothed, Lord Chayle, may come into this room at any moment, and in your present uncomfortable situation you may prefer not to have a stranger presented to you. I do not think I would, in the circumstances."

Chloe was staring at her. "Did you say 'Lord Chayle'?

"Yes, I did. Are you acquainted with him?"

"We've met," Chloe said briefly, "but I've no wish to renew my acquaintance with him or with any other gentleman while looking and feeling as I do at this moment. By all means let us go upstairs."

She put down the empty glass and rose to her feet, but was obliged to clutch at the chair for support. Sarah, clasping her by the arm, decided to let the question of Miss Frensham's acquaintance with Chayle pass for the moment.

"Come, lean on me," she said encouragingly. We have only to go through the coffee room and up the stairs."

Rather shakily, Chloe obeyed. In the coffee room, Mr. Roman was no longer to be seen, but two strangers were sitting by the fire; the elder of the two, a small, wiry man with iron-grey hair and the appearance of a respectable tradesman, got up and addressed Miss Frensham with fatherly concern.

"Feeling better, ma'am? Nasty shock for a lady, that was, the coach overturning, let alone having to tramp all that way in the snow."

"Thank you, I am much better," she replied unsteadily, "and thank you, too, for all your help. You were very kind."

"A pleasure, ma'am. A real pleasure," he assured her, and went to open the farther door for them. "Now you get a good night's sleep, and you'll be as right as a trivet in the morning."

Just outside the room they met Lucy, coming in answer to Sarah's summons. She at once took her mistress's place at Chloe's side, saying encouragingly that they would soon have her tucked up warm in bed, but as the three of them reached the angle of the passage where it turned sharply to the left to the foot of the stairs, they heard someone descending and a moment later found themselves face to face with Justin. He looked startled and made as though to step aside; then suddenly his expression changed.

"Chloe Frensham!" he exclaimed. "Good God! what are you doing here?"

The abruptness of the greeting, and the tone in which it was uttered, astonished Sarah, for she had never expected to find Chayle lacking in civility. She said reprovingly:

"Miss Frensham was travelling on the London stage, which met with an accident half a mile from here. She is feeling not at all the thing, and Lucy and I are about to help her to bed."

The cold, frowning glance rested for a moment on her face. He said, in a voice which matched it for coolness: "I feel sure that your abigail is more than capable of performing that task unaided. Let us go back to the parlour, where, I believe, dinner is about to be served."

Sarah's astonishment increased, becoming tinged with embarrassment at this lack of courtesy. "Dinner has been put back a trifle, my lord, owing to the unexpected arrival of so many other guests. I have time to see Miss Frensham comfortably settled."

"Miss Frensham will excuse you, I am sure, and yield to my prior claim upon your company." Pointedly, he moved away from the foot of the stairs, leaving the way clear, and offered Sarah his arm. There was the same implacable note in his voice that she had heard at Lady Bellingham's. "Come, Miss Lorymer."

She was tempted to defy him, but realised in time the impropriety of indulging in an argument in a public place. Casting him a furious glance, she said to Lucy:

"Take Miss Frensham upstairs, then, and be sure that she has everything she needs." To Chloe herself, she added: "I will come up after we have dined to see how you go on, and meanwhile, do not hesitate to tell Lucy what you require."

Having made this stand for independence, she allowed Justin to lead her away, and as he did so she fancied she heard Chloe Frensham give the ghost of a chuckle. In stony silence they returned to the parlour, and immediately they were inside the door she took her hand from his arm and turned to face him, but he spoke before she had an opportunity to say any of the things she had been rehearsing during the past couple of minutes. His remark was brief and dictatorial.

"Chloe Frensham is not a fit companion for you. Pray oblige me by having nothing more to do with her."

She eyed him resentfully. "That would be a trifle difficult, my lord, since I have arranged with Mrs. Ashlock that she shall share my bedchamber."

"You have done what?" he demanded incredulously, adding before she could reply: "I forbid it."

Sarah gasped. "You cannot be serious! The poor woman has had a shocking experience and was carried into this room unconscious. You saw for yourself that she could not walk upstairs unaided, and yet you take this absurd notion into your head that it will not do for us to share a room."

"It will not do. Some other arrangement must be made."

"What other arrangement, pray?" Sarah asked sharply. "There can scarcely be more than half a dozen bedchambers available in a house of this size, and there are all the stagecoach passengers to be ac-

commodated, as well as ourselves and Mr. Roman.
I have no objection to sharing my room with Miss
Frensham, who appears to me to be quite unexcep-
tionable, and since you are obviously acquainted
with her—!"

"I am acquainted with any number of persons,
ma'am, whom I would not dream of presenting to
you. Chloe Frensham is an actress, one of the lesser
lights of the Drury Lane Theatre."

"An actress?" Sarah was momentarily diverted.
"So that is why her face seemed familiar to me, although she insisted we had never met. I must have
seen her upon the stage." She dwelt on that thought
for a moment, trying to recall the occasion, but then
abandoned the attempt and returned to more pressing matters. "Well, that is neither here nor there! I
do not see what bearing it has upon the matter we
were discussing—unless, of course, you fear that
she may arouse in me the desire to become an actress, too."

"Pray do not be absurd!" he said coldly. "It is
out of the question that this woman should share
your room. The mere thought of so close and inti-
mate a contact between you is offensive."

"Not to me," she retorted angrily. "I am, I hope,
capable of putting sympathy for another's misfortune above arrogance and stupid prejudice. Miss
Frensham is quite worn out, and shockingly chilled,
and having undertaken to share my room with her I
refuse to subject her to the discomfort and indignity
of waiting while another is prepared for her. It
would be brutal to do so."

"Arrogant, prejudiced, and now brutal!" he said furiously. "Can you find no other shortcomings, ma'am, to lay at my door?"

"What else can I think," she retorted, "when you raise such trivial objections to my offering help and comfort to someone in distress? I realise that in the ordinary way Miss Frensham and I would not become acquainted, but in these circumstances I do not see why you should think it so dreadful. After all, there must be any number of perfectly respectable people in the theatrical profession."

"Possibly, but Chloe Frensham is not one of them! To put the matter bluntly, ma'am, she is a member of what I am sure you have heard those graceless brothers of yours refer to as 'the muslin company,' and my own acquaintance with her arises from the fact that until a few months ago, one of my oldest friends had her in keeping." He watched, with grim satisfaction, the blush of embarrassment which rose in Sarah's cheeks, and then added ironically: "I am sure you will forgive my lack of delicacy in referring to these matters. You are, as I recollect, an advocate of such plain speaking."

This mocking, indirect reference to their quarrel over Helena Maitland, far from adding to Sarah's discomfiture, vexed her so much that she forgot to be embarrassed. With her cheeks still becomingly flushed, and her eyes sparkling with anger, she retorted:

"And you, my lord, are shockingly inconsistent! Or would you also forbid me to share a room with

Mrs. Maitland, if she found herself in the same uncomfortable predicament as Miss Frensham?"

To her astonishment, for she had never expected to get the best of the argument, she saw that he could find no answer to this. Or, at least, no answer which dignity and decorum permitted him to make, though the look on his face suggested that there were many things he would like to have said. Sarah made haste to press the advantage she had gained.

"I cannot, of course, prevent you from forbidding her to share my room, but do not expect me to take the blame for such shockingly callous behaviour. If you wish her to be accommodated elsewhere in the house, you must tell Mrs. Ashlock so yourself, and as by this time Lucy will have the poor woman tucked up in bed, that will cause a great to-do and present you to everyone here in a most unfavourable light. I expect, however, that the opinion of mere rustics and common stagecoach travellers is of no account whatsoever to you, so you will not hesitate to give the necessary orders."

With that, and as an indication that she was washing her hands of the whole affair, she went to sit by the fire, picking up a periodical from a side table on the way, and turning the pages with every appearance of lively interest. Inwardly she was quaking, for though indignation at his intolerance and high-handedness had enabled her to defy him, she was already regretting one remark. What in the world had possessed her to mention Helena Maitland? He had assured her that the association had ended, but might he not be tempted to renew it if his intended bride cast the affair up at him every time they had a disagreement? She continued to turn the pages of the magazine, but saw nothing of what was printed upon them as she waited apprehensively for him to speak.

Justin, however, was for once unsure of himself. The thrust about Mrs. Maitland had struck home, for though one did not commonly compare a woman of birth and fortune with a Cyprian like Chloe Frensham, he could see that a gently reared girl like Sarah would have difficulty in perceiving any difference. Then, too, there was the point she had made concerning the probable result of a demand that Miss Frensham be found other accommodation, a point which he had hitherto overlooked. Even if he did not divulge the reason for such a demand, Mrs. Ashlock was shrewd enough to guess it, and would almost certainly make things very unpleasant for the luckless Chloe, towards whom Justin felt no personal ill will.

He looked with exasperation at his betrothed, still apparently engrossed in the periodical, and remembered that when he offered for her he had believed that though she might bore him, she would never irritate him. Events had proved the opposite to be the case, but he realised suddenly that the Sarah Lorymer who had been revealed during the past twenty-four hours had caught his interest in a way that the docile, self-effacing nonentity he had proposed to could never have succeeded in doing. She had not endeared herself to him, but he found it impossible any longer to regard her with indifference.

"Very clever, Miss Lorymer," he said at last. "You have succeeded in prolonging this argument to a point where, as you so obligingly point out, it would be exceedingly difficult for me to countermand the arrangement you have made. I am not, I trust, callous, and though I care very little for what our fellow guests may think, I have no desire to make things uncomfortable for Chloe Frensham, or to exacerbate an already difficult situation. I cannot like the association between you, but for the moment we will say no more about it. Let us hope that it will not need to extend beyond tonight."

Chapter VII

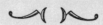

His lordship's hope proved vain. For most of the night the blizzard continued, and by morning, when it had finally blown itself out, drifts were piled high against the walls of the inn, and no carriage could possibly have passed along the road outside. The clouds still hung low and sullen, big with the threat of more snow, and there was nothing in the desolate prospect which greeted the eyes of the stranded travellers to suggest any immediate chance of continuing their various journeys.

Sarah, having retired early to bed, was up betimes, and, going down alone to the parlour, found the coffee room empty except for a boy of about eleven years old, who stood looking out of the window into the stable yard. He glanced round when he heard the door open, and revealed a round, freckled, snubnosed face below a thatch of ginger hair. It was a face which looked as though mischief usually dwelt in it, but just now it wore a subdued and doleful look, while the fact that his good suit of clothes was obviously new and, just as obviously, mourning, roused Sarah's ready sympathy. She gave him a friendly smile, and said brightly:

"Good morning. I see that the snow has stopped at last."

"Yes, ma'am," he stammered, eyeing her with considerable wariness. "Good morning, ma'am."

"You must have been travelling on the stage-coach," Sarah pursued. "I should have found it horridly frightening when it overturned, but I dare say you enjoyed it excessively."

"Yes, ma'am," he said again, looking with wonder at a lady who could appreciate his natural reaction to so exciting an event, "but now they say we must wait here until the road be clear, and there's naught to do. I wanted to help shovel snow in the yard, but Uncle Chebworth says I'll spoil my good clothes, and my old 'uns be all in the box we had to leave with the coach."

Sarah, realising what was expected of her, rose valiantly to the occasion and agreed that to be deprived of so congenial an occupation as snow-shovelling for so trifling a cause was exceedingly tire-some. She then inquired the name of her young ac-quaintance, learned that it was Toby Dilke, and was further informed that, Toby's widowed mother hav-ing recently died, "Uncle Chebworth" was taking him to live at his farm beyond Canterbury. Warm-ing to his theme, and having overcome his initial shyness, Toby then confided that he was not altogether happy at this prospect, having, as he put it, 'allus lived in a town, with streets and shops and people all about!'

"Well, no doubt you will find it a little strange at first," Sarah said encouragingly, "but a farm is a delightful place to live, you know. Until quite lately, I had always lived in the country, and I enjoyed it very much."

He eyed her mistrustfully. "On a farm?"

"Well, no, but there were several farms close by. I am sure you will come to like it, once you grow accustomed, and think of all the interesting things you will learn, which you would have no opportunity to do in a town. Your uncle will want you to help him with the animals, I expect."

Toby seemed unconvinced. "All he wants me to do is keep quiet and mind my manners. That's what he's been telling me to do ever since Ma died." He returned abruptly to his original grievance. "What harm could it do to let me help shovel snow? Even that little shaver is out there."

Looking in the direction indicated by Toby's pointing finger, Sarah saw that while a youth of about seventeen, who, from the strong family resemblance, must be yet another Ashlock, was engaged in clearing pathways from the house to the stables and other outbuildings, in one corner of the yard a stout infant, warmly muffled in coats and shawls, was solemnly imitating him, using a piece of flat wood as a shovel, and greatly hampered by the antics of a mongrel puppy which was leaping about him. Before she could reply, however, the door of the coffee room opened again and a man's voice spoke in the deep, slow accents of a countryman.

"Now then, nevvy, stop pestering the lady with your impudence. Go and sit down and wait for your breakfast." As Toby reluctantly obeyed, the speaker turned to Sarah. "Asking your pardon, ma'am. The lad don't mean no harm, but he's a sight too free in his ways, not having had a father to make him mind since he were a baby."

Sarah looked with interest at the newcomer. He seemed a typical farmer, burly, ruddy-cheeked, dressed in good broadcloth, and, far from being the peevish martinet Toby had hinted at, he looked kindly, though a trifle harassed.

"There is no need to apologise," she said with a smile. "It was I who engaged your nephew in conversation, not the other way about, and I assure you that no fault could have been found with his manners."

The farmer sighed. "Very obliging of you to say so, ma'am," he replied heavily. "The truth is, I'm not used to dealing with young 'uns, me and my good wife never being blessed with any of our own. I don't want to be hard on the lad, for he's just lost his Ma, but have him playing pranks I will not. Though how I'm to prevent it, now he has to stay kicking his heels here, is more than I can tell."

Sarah did not hesitate. "Forgive me, Mr.— Chebworth, is it not? I have no right to interfere, but might it not perhaps be better to let Toby help, as he wishes to do? I dare say Mrs. Ashlock could find him something to wear, and the work would keep him occupied and make him healthily tired. Time is likely to hang heavily for all of us, and especially for a lively boy of his age."

Mr. Chebworth looked much struck. "Well, if you think so, ma'am. 'Tis true the devil finds mischief for idle hands." He appeared to come to a sudden decision. "I'll have a word with young Joe Ashlock and see what he says."

He broke off abruptly, for Justin had just come into the room, immaculately attired in a perfectly fitting, bottle-green riding coat, buckskin breeches, and glossy top-boots. He nodded civilly in response to Mr. Chebworth's respectful "good morning, my lord," ignored Toby, who was staring at him open-mouthed, and, having greeted his betrothed, expressed a polite hope that she found herself fully recovered from the fatigues of the previous day.

By the time she had replied he had ushered her into the parlour, where, closing the door behind them, he added in the same tone of polite inquiry:

"Is it your custom, ma'am, to enter into conversation with ill-bred strangers in the public rooms of inns?"

She gasped, but made a quick recovery. "And is it your custom, my lord, to be so insufferably haughty? Mr. Chebworth is a very worthy, respectable man." She stopped abruptly, bit her lip, then added in a tone of the deepest mortification: "Oh, dear! I had quite made up my mind not to quarrel with you today."

The conclusion was so unexpected, and her look

of vexation and self-reproach so comical, that Justin's sense of the ridiculous betrayed him, and he found it impossible not to laugh.

"A commendable resolution, ma'am, and one which I am doing nothing to help you to keep," he said frankly. "Let us forget my unfortunate remark, and to make amends I will concede that there is probably no harm at all in your bucolic acquaintance, and that I only objected because I am intolerably high in the instep."

She chuckled responsively, but said quickly: "Oh, I did not really mean that! I think you have not, perhaps, been much in the way of conversing with people of that sort, and so thought it odd in me to do so, but it was the boy, Toby, whom I spoke to first. He looked so downcast, and I could not help noticing that he is in mourning, and I just *could* not walk past him without a word." She paused, looking rueful, and then added with a sigh: "I had better confess at once, my lord, that one of my besetting faults is that I cannot bear to see anyone unhappy or in trouble, and not try to help them. Mama is forever scolding me about it."

"Without reason, surely? Warmheartedness is scarcely a fault." He was still watching her, the smile lingering in his eyes. "Chloe Frensham last night, an unhappy schoolboy this morning. You are very warmhearted, Sarah, are you not?"

Colour rushed into her cheeks, and she cast him a startled, doubtful glance, confused by his sudden, unexpected use of her Christian name and not knowing whether he was teasing her or simply being sarcastic. Well aware of her uncertainty, and amused by it, he added, with a touch of assumed hauteur:

"You do not, I trust, object to my addressing you by your given name? I recollect that I have not asked your leave to use it."

The deep blush remained in her cheeks, but she answered with a dignity which both surprised and pleased him. It was a quality he had not observed in her before.

"You have every right to use it, my lord, if you wish. I gave you that right on the day I accepted your offer of marriage. As for Miss Frensham and Toby, I am sorry if my attitude towards them displeases you, but if, as you said, we are to know each other better, I cannot pretend to agree with you in everything. That would be dishonest."

"It would also be excessively tedious," he said humorously, "though I admit, until a very short time ago I thought it likely that you would do so. I judged you superficially, and can blame no one but myself for being mistaken."

She could think of only one thing to say. "I am sorry, my lord."

He looked surprised. "I said 'mistaken,' Sarah, not 'disappointed.' I believe I may frequently be angry with you, but I am now tolerably certain that I will never be bored. And I have a name, too, you know. It would please me if you could bring yourself to use it occasionally, instead of my title."

This time she could find nothing to say. The suggestion that she should address him as "Justin," even though this was how he had long figured secretly in her thoughts, was one to which she could not immediately respond, while the hint implicit in his previous remark, that her recent behaviour had not, after all, sunk her beyond reproach in his opinion, made her feel quite lightheaded with relief. He regarded her for a moment or two in a quizzical manner, then, still looking amused, inquired if Miss Frensham would be joining them for breakfast.

"Well, no!" Sarah replied, seizing eagerly upon this less personal topic. "I have had Lucy carry a tray upstairs for her. The truth is, I did not know whether you would wish her to use the parlour, and Mrs. Ashlock would think it odd if she sat down in the coffee room with the men, so—!"

"So you decided to prevaricate, in the hope of persuading me into permitting her to share this room as well as your bedchamber? Well, I have no *wish* for her to invade our privacy, but I can see that it will be thought odd if she does not, and since we are likely to be stranded here for several days, the less awkward the situation can be made, the better it will be for all of us. You *had* realised, had you not, that there is at present not the smallest hope of returning to London? A carriage could not get ten yards along the road, and, from the look of the sky, there is more snow to come."

"I know," she said guiltily, "and, I assure you, I am excessively sorry."

"I expect you are," Justin agreed dryly, "but I feel impelled to point out to you that the present situation is entirely of your contriving, and any tedium you have to endure is really no more than you deserve."

She looked quickly up at him, her eyes wide with astonishment. "Oh, *I* shall not be bored! I never am. It is on your account that I am sorry, for I *know* that you are going to find it dreadfully tedious here, with nothing to entertain you, and I am very conscious that I am to blame for that."

She sounded so anxious that he could not resist saying, in an ill-used tone: "Undoubtedly you are, and it is therefore incumbent upon you to find some means of diverting me."

"Yes, but I do not know how gentlemen usually entertain themselves all day. Perry and Charlie seem to spend a great deal of time gaming." She brightened as a sudden thought occurred to her. "Perhaps Mr. Roman plays cards. He appears to be a very fashionable young man."

"So he may, but I have no desire to spend the whole day at the gaming table."

"Well, I did not mean all day, but perhaps for an hour or two?"

"Perhaps," he conceded, "but that still leaves a good deal of time unaccounted for."

"Miss Frensham will join us later," she suggested hopefully, "and I am sure she knows how to be far more entertaining than I could ever hope to be."

"I doubt that very much. Your company, my dear Sarah, has all the charm of the unexpected. I never know what you are going to say next."

She looked doubtful. "Have I said something I should not?"

"Not at all. It is, perhaps, a trifle unusual to offer one's affianced husband a young woman of Chloe Frensham's reputation as a means of beguiling the time, but——!"

"Oh, I did not!" She coloured up again, but laughter bubbled in her voice in spite of all her efforts to keep it prim. "It is quite shocking of you to suggest that I did."

"Beyond reproach," he agreed promptly. "You see what a disastrous effect your own outspokenness has had upon me. Now, since we are to be spared Miss Frensham's company on this occasion at least, I shall ring for breakfast immediately. I understand that the house is amply provisioned, so we need not fear short commons in addition to our other ills."

"I know you do not like her," Sarah remarked, seating herself in the chair he had drawn out for her, "but one must feel for her in her present predicament. She told me that almost everything she owns is in that stagecoach, so imagine what a worry that must be, and how uncomfortable for her to be stranded here without so much as a clean handkerchief to call her own."

"An unhappy situation indeed," Justin agreed, but he spoke rather absently, his mind busy suddenly with certain curious aspects of Chloe's presence which annoyance that she was there at all had hitherto prevented him from considering. What had brought her along the Dover road in the depths of winter, with "almost all she owned," and why, in Heaven's name, by stagecoach? She had always been able to command comfort if not luxury, and though during the past few months she had dropped out of the more fashionable circles of the *demi-monde*, it was hard to believe that she found herself wholly without resources.

Breakfast was brought in by Polly Ashlock and another young woman whom Sarah addressed as "Eliza." Observing this, Justin remarked, when they were alone again, that she had been quick to familiarise herself with the names of the inn servants.

"Yes, but I believe that none of them are servants in the sense that you mean," Sarah replied. "Mrs. Ashlock has three sons—Joseph, Clem, and Robin—and Eliza is Joseph's wife. The inn is very much a family affair."

"So I perceive. Would it be imprudent of me to inquire how you so quickly discovered the ramifications of this formidable family tree?"

Sarah laughed. "Oh, from Lucy, my maid. She is a country girl herself, and has struck up a friendship with Polly Ashlock." She leaned towards him across the table, and added confidentially: "She also told me that there is something odd about one of the stagecoach passengers. His name is Layton, and Lucy and Polly are convinced that he harbours some guilty secret. He was up this morning long before anyone else, and actually tried to persuade Joe Ashlock to hire him a horse so that he could continue his journey. In this weather! Lucy says he is as nervous as a cat."

"Undoubtedly a desperate criminal flying the

country," Justin said with some amusement. "I will remember to take particular note of Mr. Layton."

An opportunity for him to do this arose later that morning. He had gone out to the stable to see for himself how the horses were housed and to have a word with Badsey, his groom, and while he was there he became aware of a mild altercation going on just outside the door.

"No, sir, I can't tell 'ee how soon the road to Dover will be open," someone was saying in the tone of one wearied by much repetition, "any more than I could tell 'ee an hour ago. The good Lord sent the snow, and He'll send the thaw when it be time for it, and all us can do is to wait."

"Damn it, man, you must be used to the weather in these parts," another voice replied irritably. "How long are the roads usually blocked? Do you think it will snow again?"

" 'Twouldn't surprise me, sir." That was the first voice, more weary than before. "It looks uncommon heavy, and that be a bad sign. Another storm like that last 'un, and you could be here for a week."

"A week?" the second voice repeated with the most profound dismay, adding, after a pause: "Is it as bad, do you think, between here and London?"

"As to that, sir, I can't say. 'Tis not likely to be much better."

"No, that's true. It is not likely."

Was there, Justin wondered, a faint note of relief in that querulous voice? He shifted his position slightly, and saw that the speaker was a man in his middle thirties, tall and rather thin, with a long, bony countenance, lank fair hair, and a harassed expression. While Justin watched him, he cast a jaundiced look at the sky, nodded lugubriously to the young Ashlock with whom he had been conversing, and plodded despondently back to the house through the slush which covered the cobbled yard where the snow had been shovelled aside. Badsey caught his lordship's eye.

"Now there's a man in a powerful hurry, my lord. Three times he's been out here, pestering one or other of the lads like that."

Justin's brows lifted. "Mr. Layton?"

"I don't know his name, m'lord. Tall, skinny fellow with a face like a tallow candle. He's properly on the fidget, and no mistake."

Justin remembered that Sarah's abigail had told her much the same thing, and wondered idly what pressing business was taking Mr. Layton to Dover —or was it just away from London? Whichever it was, he was fretting himself to no purpose; the snow would not melt any quicker because of his impatience.

When Justin returned to the inn, he found that Chloe Frensham had at last emerged from seclusion, and was sitting alone in the parlour. Not all Lucy's efforts had succeeded in removing from her fashionable gown the effects of its soaking the previous night, but otherwise she appeared to be fully recovered. She and Chayle had had some slight acquaintance while she was living under the protec-

tion of his friend, and she greeted him coolly, with
only the merest hint of defiance. He returned the
greeting, adding ironically:

"I am happy to see that you have suffered no ill
effects from your disagreeable experience."

"You are not happy to see me at all," she retorted with brutal candour. "If I know anything of the
matter, you have been wishing me elsewhere ever
since you learned that Miss Lorymer had befriend-
ed me, but don't worry, my lord. I'm actress enough
to play the lady when it's needful, and I won't do
anything, or say anything to her, that goes beyond
the line of what is proper."

Justin regarded her thoughtfully. "Do you know,
Chloe, I am inclined to believe you mean that?"

"So you may, for it's the truth. I like Miss
Lorymer, and I'm grateful to her. There are not
many ladies of quality who would have treated me
as civilly as she has done, for I've no doubt you
warned her against me—and small blame to you
for that, things being as they are. But she has a truly
kind heart."

"She has indeed. She tells me that you are in the
uncomfortable situation of having all your worldly
possessions aboard the stagecoach which is at present buried in a snowdrift somewhere along the road."

She eyed him rather warily. "That's true enough,
and a fine state they will be in when I get them
back! If I ever do!"

"I see no reason why you should not, since in this
weather nobody is likely to be out rifling the coach.

But how is this? Are you leaving the theatre and depriving your admirers of any further opportunity of seeing you upon the stage?"

She shrugged, turning a little from him and holding out one hand to the fire by which she sat. "Oh, I shall never be a great actress and I am tired of being an indifferent one. It's ten years now since I ran away from home to join a travelling company but now I'm going back."

"What a charming surprise for your family! I am sure they will welcome you with open arms."

She cast him a flashing glance from her very fine blue eyes. "Damn your mockery! If I choose to go home that's my business."

"Oh undoubtedly! Where, incidentally, is your home?"

"In a little village near Canterbury." Chloe was looking into the fire again and spoke carelessly. "You would not know it."

"I expect not," Justin agreed cordially and strolled across to stand by the fire, resting one arm along the mantelpiece. "So you are abandoning the gaiety of London in favour of the simple rural life! One can well understand the lure of the countryside, especially at this time of year." He paused expectantly, but she refused to rise to the bait, and, after cynically studying her for a few moments, he added in his driest tone: "Doing it rather too brown, Chloe! What is it really? Debts?"

"What if it is?" she retorted insolently. "Will you settle them for me?"

His brows lifted. "Hardly, my dear. I am not a philanthropist."

"I wouldn't expect you to be." She looked up at him again, a bold, inviting stare this time. He met it with a look of complete indifference, and after a second or two she laughed with a hint of regret. "No, you never did spare a glance in my direction, more's the pity! Well, my lord, I'm not running from my creditors, and I shan't try to borrow money from Miss Lorymer, if that is what is worrying you."

"Not in the least," he assured her with a touch of amusement. "It would do you no good if you did, for I fancy Miss Lorymer herself is none too plump in the pocket just at present."

She frowned with some impatience. "If you are not concerned on her behalf, why are you so damnably interested in my affairs?"

"Curiosity, my dear Chloe," he replied lightly. "I never cease to wonder at the vagaries of my fellow men—and women."

"Perhaps you are not the only one to do so. One might wonder, for example, just what *you* are doing in this place—with Miss Lorymer."

"One might," he agreed levelly, but there was an edge to his voice that she could not misunderstand. "One is at liberty, of course, to wonder what one chooses. It only becomes an impertinence when such speculation is noised abroad."

She shifted uncomfortably in her chair, and turned from him with an ill-humored shrug. Justin ignored this, for he had just become aware of

Sarah's voice in the coffee room, mingled with childish laughter and the high-pitched yelping of a dog. With a sense of deep foreboding, his lordship crossed the parlour and softly opened the door.

Chapter VIII

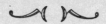

An animated scene met his eyes. Sarah was seated
on a settle by the fire, holding on her lap a stout,
flaxen-haired infant who bounced delightedly and
emitted the shrieks of mirth which had first caught
Justin's attention, while young Toby Dilke, on
hands and knees in front of them, engaged in a
mock ferocious romp with a puppy of dubious lin-
eage. The group was being watched, indifferently,
by John Roman, and benevolently by a small, wiry,
grey-haired man who was obviously another passen-
ger from the stagecoach.

In the few moments while Justin surveyed the
scene before his presence was discovered, it seemed
to him that Sarah was deriving as much pleasure
from the game as Toby and the child. Her dark
curls were a trifle ruffled, and there was a becoming
colour in her cheeks; she was laughing at the puppy's antics, and, as Justin watched, she bent her

head to whisper something in her small friend's ear, something which prompted a series of fat chuckles and a clapping together of chubby hands. Then as though becoming aware of another presence in the room, she looked up to meet his lordship's quizzical regard. The colour in her cheeks deepened perceptibly, so that she looked both disconcerted and guilty.

"Oh dear!" she said in dismay. "I thought you had gone out to look at the horses."

"You were quite right, but, having looked at them, I returned." Justin strolled forward to stand before the fire. "It would appear, however, that you have been reasonably well entertained in my absence."

He became conscious of the fact that an uncomfortable silence had settled upon the room. Toby had scrambled up, clutching the panting, wriggling puppy in his arms, and the little boy on Sarah's lap was solemn now, staring owlishly at his lordship with very round blue eyes. Mr. Roman had returned to the perusal of a newspaper already several days old, while the other man was busy packing tobacco into the bowl of a long clay pipe.

"It is also painfully clear," Justin continued pleasantly, "that my arrival has cast a blight upon the company. Permit me to inform you, Miss Lorymer, that the younger of your two gallants has a singularly unnerving stare."

Sarah chuckled. "How absurd you are! This is Mrs. Ashlock's little grandson, Billy, and he is staring at you because he has not seen you before and is inclined to be shy of strangers. He was just the same with me at first."

"An obstacle which you obviously had no difficulty in overcoming. Forgive my curiosity, but is there any particular reason why you should be in charge of Mrs. Ashlock's little grandson?"

Sarah looked him straight in the eye. "Yes, there are several. I am exceedingly fond of children. I have nothing whatsoever to do. Mrs. Ashlock, Eliza, and Polly scarcely know which way to turn with the inn so full of guests, and Billy and the puppy were very much in the way in the kitchen."

"The puppy, too? Are you also exceedingly fond of dogs?"

"I am, as it happens, but the puppy is in Toby's care, not mine. Mrs. Ashlock has very kindly made him a present of the little dog. We have been trying to think of a name for it, since it has not yet been given one, but we cannot seem to hit upon anything that suits."

His lordship contemplated the nameless one. Its parentage was obviously shrouded in mystery, for it appeared to have been put together, rather carelessly, from scraps of many different breeds. As yet it was small, but enormous paws gave promise of size to come; its coat was shaggy; its ears appeared to be odd; and its elegant, plumy tail looked as though it belonged by right to a different and far more aristocratic dog.

"I can appreciate the difficulty," Justin said at length. "It is hard to know *what* to call such a tatterdemalion."

"But that is the very thing!" Sarah exclaimed. " 'Tatters'! What could be more appropriate? Well, Toby?"

The boy nodded eagerly. "Oh yes, ma'am! If you say so."

"I hesitate to cast a rub in the way," Justin remarked, "but is the boy's uncle aware of the proposed addition to his household?"

"Of course he is," Sarah replied indignantly. "Toby would not have accepted the puppy without Mr. Chebworth's permission."

"And he gave it? You astonish me, ma'am—or was it your doing?"

"Well," she admitted mischievously, "I will confess that at first he did not view the prospect with much enthusiasm, but I contrived to persuade him."

"Yes," he said in an amused tone, "I thought you might have done. It is to be hoped that Chebworth never has cause to regret the day he made your acquaintance."

Polly came in, bearing a laden tray towards the parlour, but paused, balancing her burden on her hip, to look anxiously at Sarah.

"I hope young Billy's not plaguing you, ma'am. He's not allowed in here in the ordinary way."

Sarah assured her that he was not, and with a rather doubtful glance at Justin, and a stern warning to her nephew to behave himself, Polly went on her way. When she had made three such journeys, however, she stopped again to inform them that the luncheon his lordship had ordered was now ready, and that Billy had better come back to the kitchen.

At this, Billy set up such a wail of protest that Sarah suggested he might perhaps stay in the coffee room in Toby's charge. Polly looked dubiously at Toby, wholly occupied with his pet, and the grey-haired man took his pipe out of his mouth to say reassuringly:

"Don't you worry, my dear. I'll keep an eye on the young shaver. I've got grandchildren of my own, and one of 'em much the age of this one. He'll be safe enough here with me."

Sarah smiled warmly upon him. "How very kind of you, Mr. Bodicote! There, Billy, you need not cry, after all. Just be a good boy and do as this gentleman tells you."

She handed over her charge, who seemed reluctant to accept the change. He stared at Mr. Bodicote with underlip outthrust until the latter produced from his pocket a large silver repeater watch, and set it striking, which so fascinated the child that he immediately forgot his grievance. Justin ushered Sarah into the parlour, but before following her, he turned and said pleasantly:

"Will you join us, Mr. Roman?"

John Roman looked surprised but gratified, and accepted the invitation with alacrity. As Justin had expected, Chloe brightened perceptibly at the addition of another gentleman to the party—one, moreover, who made no secret of his appreciation of her charms—and the next hour or so passed pleasantly enough. During that time, they noticed that it had begun to snow again, not fiercely now, but steadily. The large flakes floated down in a gentle, almost lazy way, which nevertheless piled the drifts still higher and began to fill the hollows between, while in the stable yard the paths so laboriously cleared that morning began to disappear again beneath a layer of white.

Inside the house it was cosy enough, with log fires blazing and, as the day began to draw in, the glow of candlelight. The atmosphere, too, was comfortable, for although any hope of soon continuing their various journeys had receded even farther, the occupants of the inn, thrown together by chance, had not yet had time to weary of one another's company. Quite the reverse, in fact, in one instance, as Justin had pointed out to him late that afternoon.

Passing through the coffee room on his way to the parlour he found the grey-haired Mr. Bodicote there alone, leaning on the back of a chair, puffing at his long clay pipe and gazing thoughtfully through the open door into the inner room. Sarah was there, sittting by the fire with little Billy Ashlock leaning against her knee; she appeared to be mending some toy, and she and the child were both intent upon it. Behind her, and a little to the right, John Roman and Chloe Frensham were seated at the table, where playing cards were scattered. Their chairs were very close together, and they were conversing under their breath, the young man's lips only an inch or two from the cluster of bright curls over Chloe's left ear.

At Justin's approach, Mr. Bodicote looked round, so obviously with the intention of speaking that his lordship paused. The other man took the pipestem from between his lips and pointed with it at the two in the parlour.

"Now there's a gent, my lord, as is in no hurry for the weather to break. Not one to waste his time, he ain't! Your lordship's acquainted with the young woman, I believe?"

Justin's brows lifted; he said, at his coldest and haughtiest: "And if I am, what is that to you?"

"No offence, my lord! No offence! I was just wondering, since you do know her, if you happen to know any of her friends?"

"And *I* am wondering what the devil you think you are about, cross-questioning me in this fashion. I do not like impertinence, my friend."

"There's none intended, my lord," Mr. Bodicote assured him. He straightened up and laid a detaining hand on Justin's sleeve as the latter started to move away. "A word with you in private, sir, if you'd be so kind."

Something in his manner caught Justin's interest and checked the frigid rebuke he had been about to utter. He shrugged slightly, and followed Bodicote as the elder man moved away to the window on the far side of the room.

"Well?" he said curtly.

Mr. Bodicote cast a wary glance in the direction of the parlour and spoke very quietly. "I'll be obliged, my lord, if you'll keep to yourself what I'm going to say. I'm an officer of the law, sir. Bow Street."

"Bow Street?" Justin repeated in astonishment. "Then what the devil——?" He broke off, frowning. "Chloe Frensham?"

"That's right, my lord," Bodicote agreed stolidly, "but it's not her I'm after as much as the man I'm hoping she'll lead me to. Name of Christopher Frome."

He looked hopefully at Justin as he spoke; Justin shook his head.

"I have never heard of him. Of what is he suspected?"

"Theft, my lord. He stole a music-box off his uncle."

"Stole a——!" Justin's frown deepened, his lips compressed. "I think you are making game of me, Bodicote. Must I warn you again that I will not tolerate impertinence?"

"It's God's truth, my lord," Bodicote assured him gloomily, "though I'm not surprised you don't believe it. I didn't believe it myself, but there it is! Young Frome up and stole this music-box from his uncle after a quarrel over some debts the lad wanted paid. The old gentleman's very rich—made a fortune out East, so I'm told—and young Frome, being his heir, has been living on his expectations ever since he came of age. Then a twelvemonth back, Uncle up and takes a young wife, and now there's a baby son and no more credit for the nevvy. No more help from his uncle, either, and that's why they quarrelled. The young fellow was ordered out of the house, and it seems the music-box went with him, so we was called in. Just spite, if you ask me! After all, what's a music-box?"

"What, indeed?" Justin agreed dryly. "Such trifles can be costly, but one would hardly suppose—! Why, I wonder, did Frome steal it in the first place? Could he lay hands on nothing more valuable?"

"More spite, seemingly, or so old Mr. Frome says. His most treasured possession, it was. Matter o' sentiment. And the lad knew it."

"A delightful family! How does Chloe Frensham come into the affair?"

"Young Frome's had her in keeping these four months past, which is one reason, I reckon, that he's got so deep in debt. Well, my lord, by the time I was put on the case the young fellow had disappeared, but according to information from his uncle, the wench'd be off to join him before long. So I kept an eye on her, and bless me if yesterday morning she didn't up and leave London, bag and baggage. So I came along as well."

"She told me this morning," Justin remarked, "that she is on her way to visit her family, near Canterbury."

Mr. Bodicote nodded. "It's Canterbury she's bound for, my lord, but it's my belief she's meeting Frome there. Or was, until this dratted snow turned everything topsy-turvy. But for that, I might have had my hand on him by now."

He fell silent, brooding, apparently, upon the malice of nature in thus abetting a criminal, and after a moment or two Justin said encouragingly:

"If your deductions are correct, Bodicote, as I fancy they may well be, this is merely an irritating delay. Frome is probably snowbound in Canterbury just as Miss Frensham is here, and they will keep their assignation as soon as it is possible to do so."

"Aye, my lord, if she don't find someone more to her taste in the meantime," Bodicote said pessimistically. "I've never known one of her sort yet as hadn't got an eye to the main chance, and Frome's pockets are still to let, without he's broke the law, stealing off his uncle." He cast another glance in the direction of the parlour. "It wouldn't surprise me to see her off back to London with *that* young spark once the weather clears, and then how am I going to find Christopher Frome?"

"You could still look for him in Canterbury," Justin suggested. "He will be seeking news of Miss Frensham, no doubt, if he is expecting her to arrive from London."

"I could, my lord, and that's what I shall have to do, but whether I'd find him or not's another matter. I've never laid eyes on him."

Justin frowned. "You have a description of him, surely?"

"Oh, yes," Mr. Bodicote said bitterly. "I'm told he's a medium-sized young fellow with dark hair. How many like that does your lordship suppose I'll see in Canterbury? Could be anybody."

"It is very little to go upon, certainly. Unhappily, I cannot assist you, for during my previous slight acquaintance with Miss Frensham, she was not liv-

ing under the protection of Christopher Frome.
However, I wish you all success."

The Runner thanked him without enthusiasm.
Justin was about to move away when another
thought struck him and he looked again at Mr. Bodicote.

"Have you any better description of the stolen ar-
ticle than you have of the thief?"

"Oh, yes, my lord, I know what *that* looks like.
It's a silver casket, about six inches by four by three,
all engraved with heathen pictures. The old gentleman brought it back from foreign parts and had it
made into a music-box. When you lift the lid,
there's a little silver nightingale inside that moves its
wings while the music plays."

Justin's brows lifted. "An expensive trifle! Perhaps young Mr. Frome was less foolish than he appeared."

"Shouldn't think so, my lord. Oh, the box is
worth a fair bit, I grant you, but it wouldn't be an
easy thing to sell, nor he wouldn't get no more than
a trifle of its real value. No, I reckon he just took it
out of spite, like his uncle said. They seem fair to
hate each other, those two."

The door from the passage opened and Mr.
Layton wandered in. There was a powdering of
snow on his shoulders, and his long, bony, sallow-
complexioned face wore an expression of profound
gloom.

"No sign of the weather improving," he announced despondently. "I've just been out in the

yard, and the snow is nearly two inches deep over the paths that were cleared this morning."

Justin, who had no intention of becoming involved in a discussion on so unprofitable a subject, inclined his head in civil acknowledgment of the information and went towards the parlour. As he did so, he heard Mr. Bodicote say briskly:

"Well, it won't stop no quicker for your looking at it, Mr. Layton, and there's no sense in standing out in the yard till you catch your death. What you need is a drop o' brandy. It'll warm you up *and* cheer you up, mark my words!"

Justin closed the door of the parlour behind him. "It is to be hoped," he remarked, "that our enforced sojourn here will not be too prolonged. If it is, I shall entertain grave fears for Layton's sanity."

John Roman laughed. "Is he the sallow-faced fellow who cannot be still? I think your lordship is too generous, for if we *are* cooped up here in his company for more than a day or so, it's my belief he will drive us all out of our minds."

"He nearly drove me out of mine on the way here," Chloe said with a shrug. "Sitting on the edge of his seat and looking at his watch every five minutes, and fidgeting about when we stopped to change horses as though he expected a clap on the shoulder at any moment. Then, when it started to snow—!" She left the sentence unfinished, and cast up her eyes in a manner which indicated that Mr. Layton's impatience defied description.

Justin looked thoughtfully at her. She was still sitting beside John, but now he was not leaning so close, and had taken up the cards to shuffle them idly, while she, an elbow on the table and her chin on her hand, watched indifferently. Justin wondered if Mr. Bodicote's suspicions were well founded, or if he had come on a fool's errand; this theory would certainly explain the more puzzling aspects of Chloe's journey, but Chayle had not been greatly impressed by the Runner himself. Probably, he reflected, the authorities at Bow Street set very little importance on what seemed to be a trifling theft, and had not seen fit to put the affair into the hands of one of their more efficient officers.

"Well, *I* am sorry for Mr. Layton!" Sarah's voice broke in upon his thoughts. "There, Billy! I have mended this for you, so take it, and run along like a good boy to find your Mama. It is plain that some urgent matter is taking him to Dover, and it must be quite dreadful to be delayed in this fashion at such a time. I do not think you should make fun of him because he is anxious."

"Miss Lorymer's kind heart again," Justin said, smiling at her. He became aware that Billy, finding the door shut and being unable to reach the latch, had fixed him with a reproachful stare, and opened it again for the child to pass through. This afforded him a glimpse of Mr. Layton standing at the window of the coffee room and gazing miserably out, even though it was now too dark to see anything but the snowflakes sliding down the glass. "We will endeavour to be charitable, then, and may succeed since we are able to avoid Layton's company. Those who cannot have my profound sympathy."

Probably it was Joe Ashlock and his brothers who stood most in need of this, since it was they who had to bear the brunt of Mr. Layton's feverish inquiries. He appeared to grow more harassed with each passing hour, and for the rest of the day could be seen prowling uneasily about, going to the door to see if it was still snowing, or poring over such information regarding stagecoach times as the Rose in Hand could offer. In the parlour Sarah and Justin, John, and Chloe talked idly together, or played cards in a lighthearted fashion for enormous, imaginary stakes; in the coffee room, Mr. Chebworth and Mr. Bodicote, each with a pipe in his hand and a tankard at his elbow, sat in companionable silence, or carried on long, slow-voiced conversations, while Toby embarked earnestly upon the training of Tatters, but Mr. Layton, it seemed, could not be still. He drifted from place to place like an unquiet spirit.

Sarah's last glimpse of him that evening came when she and Chloe passed through the coffee room on their way to bed, the two gentlemen having settled down in earnest to cards. Chebworth and Bodicote were still chatting by the fire, but the younger man sat apart, still at the table in the middle of the room where he had eaten his dinner. He sprawled in his chair, and a glass and a half-empty bottle on the table before him offered a silent explanation of this unwonted passivity. His chin was sunk on his chest, and though he looked up beneath his brows as the two young women passed him, his glance was hazy and he gave no other acknowledgment of their presence.

Next morning, Sarah was dressed before Chloe and went downstairs alone. It had stopped snowing and the sky was clearer, but it was freezing hard and there was clearly no possibility of yet leaving the inn. She wondered how Mr. Layton would sustain another day of inactivity. If he again had recourse to the bottle, it seemed likely that by the time travel was once more possible, he would be in no fit state to resume his journey.

At the foot of the stairs, where the passage turned sharply to the right towards the coffee room, Tatters was worrying at a door in the angle of the wall. He pranced forward with wagging tail to greet her but returned immediately to the door, first sniffing loudly at the crack beneath it, then whining and scratching at the wood. Since a door in that position could lead only to a cupboard, Sarah ordered him firmly to come away, but he would pay no heed.

"Very well, you horrid, disobedient little dog," she informed him severely, "I shall not try any more to save you from getting into trouble. Stay there until your master comes."

She was about to go on her way when she realized that Toby was nowhere to be seen. This was odd, since the previous day he had refused to be parted for a moment from his pet, and it suddenly occurred to Sarah that he might, in play with the pup, have hidden himself in the cupboard. The door was fastened on the outside by a latch which could conceivably have dropped into place of its own accord, and in some concern she thrust the puppy aside and lifted it, intending to give Toby, if he should be inside, a stern lecture on the folly of such pranks.

The instant the catch was released, the door began to swing open, impelled by some heavy object pressing against it from within. Sarah tried to hold it, but the weight was beyond her strength and she was obliged to step quickly back as the door swung irresistibly towards her. Tatters fled, yelping, and from inside the cupboard the figure of a man toppled slowly forward and rolled onto the floor at her feet. A small man with iron-grey hair, his face so blackened and horribly distorted that it was scarcely recognizable.

Chapter IX

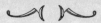

Sarah stood frozen, staring down at the body at her feet. She wanted to scream, to faint, to run, to do anything but continue to look at those swollen, discoloured features, but she was gripped by a paralysis of horror, and not one muscle of her body would obey the dictates of her will. Not until she heard Chayle's voice somewhere above, exchanging a civil good morning with one of their fellow guests, did the bonds of shock loosen a little. She still could not tear her gaze away, but she managed to utter his name, first in a kind of strangled croak, and then again, more distinctly, in a rising scream of sheer terror.

She heard him come plunging recklessly down the stairs, rap out an incredulous oath as he reached her, and then she was in his arms with her face buried against his coat, so that, mercifully, the horror was hidden from her at last. Heavier footsteps sounded on the stairs, and a babble of alarmed and inquiring voices from various directions. Justin said sharply:

"For God's sake, Chebworth, cover that before the other women come! Pull down the curtain over there. That will serve."

There was the rattle of curtain rings and the sound of ripping cloth as this command was hastily obeyed. Mr. Chebworth said in a shaken voice:

"By God, my lord, this be murder!"

"So I perceive!" Justin spoke very grimly. "Be good enough to remain here for a few minutes, and allow no one to interfere. Oh, and send Miss Lorymer's maid to the parlour with a glass of brandy. I will be back directly."

He lifted Sarah bodily in his arms and carried her along the passage and through the coffee room into the parlour. She had not made a sound since she cried his name, but she was shuddering so violently that he was considerably alarmed, and when he would have set her down in one of the big chairs by the fire her clutch upon him tightened too desperately to be easily broken. He sat down himself, still holding her.

"Sarah," he said gently. "My poor dear, you have had a terrible shock, but it is over now. Try to compose yourself."

She appeared to make a tremendous effort to do so, and said in a trembling whisper: "Tatters was scratching the cupboard door. I thought Toby might have hidden himself inside, and the catch dropped, so I opened it." Another violent shudder shook her, but she lifted her head to look at him, her eyes enormous in her white face. "Justin, was it ... was it Mr. Bodicote?"

"I fear so," he replied gravely, "but try not to dwell upon the thought of it, though that is not easy, I know." He paused, looking searchingly at her. "Sarah, believe me, I would have given anything in the world to spare you the shock of such a discovery."

A faint tinge of colour crept into her pallid cheeks, and she struggled to sit upright, suddenly shy of being held so closely in his arms. "It was nobody's fault but my own. The shock of finding— that, was horrible, but truly, I am better now. Should you not go back? No one will have the least idea what to do."

"I am by no means certain that *I* have," he replied in a wry tone, "and I certainly have no intention of leaving you alone. Whatever has happened, and whatever has to be done, *you* are my first concern."

As he spoke, he realized with surprise that this was absolutely true, and not merely from a sense of duty. His first reaction to the shocking discovery had been, not that a man was violently dead, but that it was Sarah who had stumbled upon the body. Now, seeing her still so white and shaken, yet trying so valiantly to recover some semblance of composure, he was strangely touched. He allowed her to rise to her feet, since this was obviously what she wished, but got up also and at once took both her cold hands in his, holding them in a comforting clasp. Her fingers clung tightly to his, but she said again, in a voice which was almost, though not quite, steady:

"You must go back. Someone will have to decide what should be done, and they are bound to look to you."

He recognized, reluctantly, the truth of her words. In the present appalling crisis—and precisely how appalling it was, was only just beginning to dawn upon him—decisions would have to be made, action taken, and Sarah was right when she said that their companions would look to him to take command. It was an obligation imposed upon him by his rank and position, however little fitted for the task he might feel himself to be.

"I will go directly Lucy comes to you, and not before. Come, sit here by the fire." He forced her gently into the chair, fetched a cushion to put behind her head, and then paused, resting one hand on the back of the chair, to cast another searching glance at her face. She was still very pale, with a look of lingering horror in her eyes, but she managed to summon up the tiny ghost of a smile, even though it wavered and vanished almost at once. His fingers brushed gently across her cheek, and he said quietly: "You are a remarkably brave girl, Sarah Lorymer."

He straightened up and turned as Lucy came hurrying in from the coffee room. She was white and shocked, but seemed more concerned for her mistress than anything else.

"Oh, my lord, what a dreadful thing!" she exclaimed. "Miss Sarah, are you all right?"

"It has been a shocking experience for her," Justin said before Sarah could reply. "You will stay
here with her, Lucy, until I come back." He took
the glass of brandy the abigail was holding, and
handed it to Sarah. "Drink this, my dear. It will
make you feel more the thing."

She made a little pleading grimace. "Must I?"

"Indeed you must," he replied, smiling. "I dare
say you may not care for it very much, but it is an
excellent restorative, and exactly what you need at
this moment." He took her free hand and lifted it
briefly to his lips. "I will come back as soon as I
can."

He went out, and along the passage to the foot of
the stairs, where he found most of the occupants of
the inn gathered in a staring, muttering group
around Mr. Chebworth, who still stood guard over
the curtain-shrouded corpse. In the background,
Eliza Ashlock was indulging in a fit of hysterics; little Billy was wailing in Polly's arms; and Tatters,
struggling and whining in Toby's grip, was adding
his mite to the commotion. When Justin appeared,
this subsided a little, and there was a general turning towards him.

"Oh, my lord, what's to be done?" Mrs. Ashlock,
abandoning Eliza, thrust her way to the front of the
group. Her high complexion had faded; she looked
white and drawn and considerably older. "There's
never been such a thing in my house before. Never!"

"That I can believe, ma'am," Justin replied
wryly. He looked about him with a frown. "The
first necessity, I believe, is to ascertain more particularly what has befallen this poor fellow. Roman,
Ashlock, perhaps you will remain to assist me. The
rest of you go to the coffee room. Is everyone here?"

There was a general murmur of assent, interrupted by Toby.

"Mr. Layton ain't, my lord."

Mrs. Ashlock sniffed. "Still asleep, most like.
Drunk as an owl last night, he was."

John Roman, standing on the lowest stair with
Chloe beside him, said sharply: "Was he not sharing a room with Bodicote?"

A ripple of uneasiness ran through the group, and
Justin's frown deepened.

"Someone had better go and see." His glance
singled out his groom among the group of men near
the kitchen door. "You, Badsey. If he is still sleeping,
rouse him and tell him to come downstairs."

"Aye, my lord."

Badsey shouldered his way forward, edged past
Chloe with a muttered apology, and disappeared
stolidly up the stairs. Justin stepped aside and ges-
tured towards the coffee room, and obediently the
company trooped past him in that direction. He de-
tained Chloe a moment to say in a low voice:

"Miss Lorymer and her maid are in the parlour.
You will probably prefer to join them."

She nodded, but moved past him like a sleep-
walker, apparently stunned by shock. When only
he, John Roman, and Joe Ashlock remained in the

passage, Justin bent and pulled aside the curtain Mr. Chebworth had spread over the body. Joe gave a smothered exclamation, and Roman lost colour and turned quickly away for a moment.

The examination of the body told them little. The unfortunate man had been strangled with his own neckcloth, which was still knotted tightly about his throat, and he had been dead for some hours. He was fully dressed, and both his purse and his watch were still in his pockets, but, to Justin's unacknowledged disquiet, there was nothing on his person to give any hint of his business or where he lived, and certainly nothing to suggest any motive for his murder.

While they were occupied with their grim task, Badsey came down the stairs to report that he had found Mr. Layton still asleep, and so heavily sunk in slumber that it had proved difficult to rouse him. However, he was awake now, and would come down as soon as he was dressed.

"Which I'd better lend him a hand to do, my lord, him looking as sick as a horse," the groom concluded. "Properly foxed he must have been last night, and no mistake."

"Very well, Badsey," Justin agreed. "Make what haste you can, for when we have finished here it will be necessary to investigate the bedchamber also, to discover if Bodicote has left anything there which may shed some light on the shocking affair." To Ashlock and Roman he added: "Whatever baggage he had with him was, I imagine, left in the coach, but he must have been wearing a greatcoat, and the pockets of that should be searched."

This, presently, was done, but yielded no result. By that time the body had been carried to an outhouse on the far side of the yard, the door of which was then securely padlocked and the key handed over to his lordship, who accepted the charge resignedly. Then, in silence, they all returned to the coffee room.

Everyone except Sarah, Chloe, and the abigail was now assembled there, including Mr. Layton, who, hurriedly dressed, unshaven, and with a greenish tinge to his complexion, sat by a table with his head resting on his hands. Chayle nodded to the company, but went on into the parlour. The three young women, who had been talking in hushed voices, looked up anxiously. Justin went across to Sarah.

"Do you feel sufficiently recovered, my dear, to come to the coffee room? It is necessary that everyone should be present."

"Yes, of course." She rose rather shakily to her feet, but paused, leaning on his supporting arm, to look anxiously up into his face. "What have you found out?"

"As yet, precisely nothing," he replied rather grimly. "We must now see whether questioning can throw any light upon what happened."

He led her into the coffee room, the others following, and John placed chairs for the two ladies while Lucy went to join Polly and Eliza. Then Justin, tak-

ing up a position in front of the fire so that he was
facing the assembled company, said without pream-
ble:

"You all know why we are here. At some time
during last night, one of our number was brutally
murdered and his corpse concealed in a place to
which everyone in the house has access. There is
nothing upon the body or among his effects to tell us
anything about the man or to suggest why the crime
was committed." He looked at the coachman, standing with his colleague, the guard, just inside the
door. "Where did Bodicote board the stage, and
where was he bound?"

The coachman scratched his head. "He got on in
London, me lord, and he was going to Canterbury."

"Travelling alone?"

"That he was, me lord. All the passengers was
singles, except for Mr. Chebworth and the lad, as
boarded us at Rochester. Half empty, we was, on
account of the weather."

Justin nodded. "Precisely! No one would be
traveling in such conditions except on pressing
business. Chebworth, you had a good deal of conversation with Bodicote. Did he throw out no hint of
what was taking him to Canterbury?"

"I'm bound to say, my lord, as he didn't," the
farmer replied regretfully: "He talked very pleasant, and very interesting, about any number of
things, but he never told me nothing about himself."

"That's odd!" John Roman remarked. "Why
should he be so dashed secretive?"

"Why should he not?" Justin asked dryly. "A

man is not obliged to discuss his business with every chance acquaintance."

"I know, but in a situation such as this it is natural to exchange such information with one's companions. I've made no secret of the fact that I am on my way back to London from my brother's wedding. You, my lord, are escorting Miss Lorymer to the bedside of a sick relative; Miss Frensham is going to visit her family; and Chebworth has been to Rochester to fetch the boy." John paused, and his glance turned meaningly towards the only remaining traveller. "We don't know, of course, about Mr. Layton."

Mention of his name caused Layton to raise his head, to find that he had become the centre of attention. The livid pallor of his face seemed to become more pronounced, and after looking about him in what Sarah could not help thinking was a hunted way, he said hoarsely:

"I've got urgent business in Dover. Personal and private business I don't intend to speak of."

John shrugged slightly and turned away, as though prevarication was no more than he had expected. Mrs. Ashlock, who appeared to have taken an aversion to Mr. Layton, gave a disparaging sniff; and Justin said quietly:

"None of us have any wish to pry into your private concerns, Layton, and I certainly have no authority to do so. Let me remind you, though, that inquiries will presently be made by those who do have such authority, and I advise you to consider carefully what answer you will make to them. Now

tell me this. You were sharing a room with Bodicote. Was he there when you went to bed?"

Mr. Layton looked more harassed than ever. "I
. . . I think so, my lord, but to tell you the truth, I
can't rightly remember."

"He were there," Joe Ashlock put in with a touch
of scorn. "Me and Mr. Bodicote had to help Mr.
Layton upstairs, him being too unsteady on his legs
to climb 'em alone, and I left 'em together. The last
I saw, Mr. Bodicote was helping him off with his
boots."

"I don't remember," Layton repeated miserably.
"I'm not used to strong drink. I don't remember
anything until your lordship's man woke me just
now and told me about this ghastly affair." He uttered a groan and bowed his head again upon his
hands. "I'll never touch brandy again!"

"Mr. Bodicote's bed hadn't been slept in," Badsey reminded them stolidly.

There was a pause. The logs on the hearth crack-
led cheerfully, but their bright glow was chilled by
the cold, white light streaming in through the windows, just as suspicion and fear had now chilled the
comfortable tolerance with which the occupants of
the inn had hitherto regarded each other, for in this
little, isolated world hemmed all about by snowdrifts, murder had struck sometime during the secret hours of the night. Sarah shivered and looked
towards Justin for reassurance, but his face was at
its most stern, the fine lips compressed and a deep
frown between the brows, so that there seemed to be

no trace left of the man who had held her and comforted her so short a time ago.

He was looking at Joe Ashlock. "Did Bodicote come downstairs again after that?

"Not that I knows of, sir," Joe replied. "It were getting late by then, and except for you and Mr. Roman in the parlour, everyone had gone to bed. Even after you two gentlemen went up I were about for a bit, making sure the fires was safe and everything locked up, and *I* never saw aught of him."

"Did anyone else?" Justin asked the company in general.

There were uneasy mutters of dissent and a shaking of heads. For a few moments he did not speak, but silently surveyed them, his frowning glance passing from one face to another. At length he shrugged.

"It is obvious," he said with cold deliberation, "that I have no choice but to accept those assurances. It is equally obvious that at least one of us is lying."

There was another murmur, this time laced with indignation, though only Chloe ventured to voice that indignation openly. She looked pale and shaken, as did all the women, and this, by some curious paradox, served to emphasize a boldness in her looks and manner which had not been evident before. It was as though the shock of what had happened had stripped away one thin veneer of her refinement.

"All very fine, my lord," she said shortly, and her voice, too, seemed a shade more strident than before, "but no good can come of making accusations like that."

Justin's cool gaze settled indifferently upon her. "It was not an accusation, Miss Frensham. It was a statement of fact. Let me remind you that we are snowbound here, and that it is as impossible for anyone to approach the inn as it is for us to leave it. Therefore Bodicote's murderer must be here, in this room."

From the appalled silence which greeted his words it was plain that this fact had not previously dawned upon all those present. Sarah, who had realized it while she sat in the parlour but had been trying not to think of it, bowed her head and stared hard at her hands, which were gripped tightly together in her lap. She was very frightened, and did not want anyone to know it.

Justin, more observant than she supposed, moved quietly to her side and laid his hand reassuringly on her shoulder. She looked quickly up at him, and after an instant's hesitation lifted her own hand to his. He took it in a comforting clasp.

Eliza was sobbing noisily, her child strained to her bosom. Mrs. Ashlock, grey-faced, said in a trembling voice:

"Heaven help us! My lord, what's to be done?"

"Unfortunately, ma'am, there is nothing at present which can be done." Justin spoke without moving from Sarah's side. "As soon as it is possible to get through to the village, the constable must be summoned, and information laid before the nearest justice. Meanwhile, all we can do is to wait."

"What for, me lord?" the coachman demanded belligerently. "For someone else to go the same way as poor Bodicote?"

"That is extremely unlikely, I imagine," Justin replied coldly, "and such a suggestion can only increase the natural fears of the women. If you have any similar thoughts in your head, be good enough to keep them to yourself."

Abashed as much by the blighting tone in which this rebuke was spoken as by the words themselves, the coachman subsided, muttering, and no one else volunteered any remark. After another comprehensive look round the room, Justin went on:

"I suggest that we all return to whatever we were doing when this shocking discovery was made. It is useless, of course, to suppose that any of us can put it out of our minds, but since it is apparently impossible to shed any light upon what happened last night, there is nothing to be gained by remaining gathered together."

"You don't mean, my lord," Mrs. Ashlock said in a shocked tone, "that we should go on as though nothing had happened, when that poor man is lying dead?"

"I fear we have no choice, ma'am," Justin replied, more kindly. "A shocking tragedy has occurred, but I am persuaded that you will find it better to be busy about your usual concerns than to sit brooding over it."

For a moment or two longer she looked at him. Then she nodded and got up from her chair.

"Your lordship's right," she said briskly. "The

work won't do itself, no matter what's happened. Eliza, stop that noise, do! Come back to the kitchen —and you, too, Polly. As for you boys, if his lordship's done with you, there's plenty of work for you outside." She bent a kindly glance upon Toby, who, big-eyed and silent, was standing beside his uncle with Tatters still clasped in his arms. "You'd best go with them, my dear. I dare say Robin could do with some help clearing the yard again."

He went eagerly enough; the coachman and guard, and the postboy, had already retreated to the taproom on the other side of the passage. Lucy said hesitantly:

"Do you want me to stay with you, miss?"

Sarah shook her head. "No, I think not, thank you. You had better go with Mrs. Ashlock."

She let Justin help her up, and went with him into the parlour. Chloe and John followed, but for a while no one spoke. Then Chloe, who had been standing by the fire, staring down into it, turned abruptly to Justin.

"What do *you* think happened last night?"

His brows lifted. "My dear ma'am, how can I say? Someone murdered Bodicote and concealed his body in a cupboard. There are ten men in the house, any one of whom is, I imagine, physically capable of the deed."

She made an impatient movement. "That is no answer. It's absurd to suppose, for instance, that you or Mr. Roman could have done it."

"We *could* have done it, Miss Frensham. It is, I own, extremely unlikely that either of us did."

"Someone did it," she retorted unanswerably, and turned to John. "What do you think? Do you suspect anyone?"

He shook his head. "As far as I can see, there's no reason to suspect one person more than another."

"No reason?" she repeated angrily. "What about that fellow Layton? He has behaved suspiciously all along—*and* he was sharing a room with Bodicote."

"And he was drunk last night," Justin reminded her in a dry tone. "Do not forget that."

"Perhaps he was only feigning drunkenness. He may think that if everyone can be made to believe that he lay all night in a stupor, he will neither be suspected of the crime nor expected to shed any light on Bodicote's actions. I tell you there is something havey-cavey about him. In the coach he was all the while on the fret because we were making such bad time, and yesterday he was as fidgety as a flea on a griddle. And why won't he say what his business is in Dover?"

"All of this may quite well have a perfectly innocent explanation," Justin told her with a hint of sternness. "Do not refine too much on his lack of candour this morning. By the look of him he was in no state to make any rational decision."

"Yes, a pretty batch he must have made of it last night," John agreed with a grin. "You must admit, though, that he is the only person here who has not beeen completely frank and open, or whose behaviour has been at all out of the common way."

Justin, remembering Mr. Bodicote's confidences

the previous day, made some mental reservations as he agreed with this, and added reasonably:

"Unless you are suggesting that Layton killed Bodicote in a fit of drunken fury, in which case he would scarcely have been capable of carrying the corpse downstairs and concealing it in the cupboard, what possible motive could he have for the crime?"

"What motive could anyone else have?" Chloe retorted. "None of us know anything at all about that poor man."

"We know one thing," Sarah put in unexpectedly. "He was a family man. Do you not remember, he said yesterday that he had grandchildren, one of them much the same age as Billy Ashlock?" Her voice broke suddenly and she turned away, covering her face with her hands. "Oh, how dreadful for his wife and children to learn that he is dead, and in so horrible a manner!"

"My dear!" Justin went to her at once, putting his arm round her and leading her to a chair by the fire. "Come, try not to distress yourself. We should not be dwelling upon the matter in this fashion, for you suffered a far worse shock than any of us, and you are still overwrought."

"Lord Chayle is right," John agreed emphatically, and directed a warning glance at Chloe. "Of course, none of us can forget what has happened, but at least we need not continue to talk of it. Dash it all, if we do, we may end by suspecting each other, and what could be more absurd than that?"

Chapter X

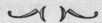

The rest of that day seemed to Sarah like a macabre charade. Everyone tried so hard to behave as though nothing had happened that every word, every gesture, every trivial action seemed exaggerated, as though they were all players upon a stage; and all the while the thought of what lay in the locked outhouse across the yard never left their minds. During the morning, Clem and Robin Ashlock set out to try to walk to the village two miles away, but the snowdrifts were waist-deep and crusted with a treacherous film of ice, and after half an hour of floundering and sliding the boys, almost frozen, were obliged to abandon the attempt.

Sarah, struggling to prevent her thoughts from constantly returning to that awful moment when she had opened the cupboard, was aware of similar tensions in her three companions. Each of them showed a tendency to lapse into abstraction and then hurriedly begin to talk of something quite trivial, as though hoping that his preoccupation would pass unnoticed; and they all watched the weather as anxiously as Mr. Layton had done the previous day. Once or twice, Chloe started to speak of the murder and of her suspicions of Layton, and each time was courteously but firmly silenced by Justin.

Justin, in fact, had even more to occupy his thoughts than the rest of them. If Bodicote had been telling the truth the previous day—and there seemed to be no possible reason for so gratuitous a falsehood—why had no proof of his identity and authority come to light? Justin knew very little of the methods employed by Bow Street, but it was inevitable that a Runner in pursuit of a criminal would be furnished with such proof, and so there was only one possible explanation of its absence. Someone now at the inn had known, or had discovered, that Bodicote was an officer of the law, and for reasons of his own had murdered him; and then, knowing nothing of Bodicote's disclosure to his lordship, had disposed of the evidence of the dead man's profession. But who? The most obvious suspect was Layton, yet there was no shred of evidence to justify making an accusation against him. So Chayle kept his own counsel, reflecting that since no one could either leave the inn or come to it, it was wiser to say nothing.

He was still more than a little concerned about Sarah. She was succeeding tolerably well in a valiant attempt to act as though nothing had happened, but the shock she had suffered that morning was not easily recovered from; she looked pale and drawn, with shadows about her eyes which made them look larger than ever, and she was inclined to start nervously at any sudden sound. She entered dutifully into the spasmodic conversation with which they strove to pass the time, and agreed, though listlessly, to take part in a game of cards, but the only thing which seemed to restore her spirits for a while was the intrusion, during the afternoon, of little Billy, who escaped from the kitchen and came in search of her, having taken a great fancy to her the previous day. Presently Toby—accompanied, inevitably, by Tatters—came to look for him, and though the company of a somewhat noisy infant, a schoolboy, and an untrained puppy was by no means to his lordship's taste, he suffered it without protest when he observed its beneficial effect upon his betrothed. He suffered it alone, for neither Chloe nor John was in the parlour. Chayle noted this mutual absence cynically and without comment, and could only be thankful that the children's presence prevented it from becoming obvious to Sarah.

For the hour or so that Toby and Billy remained with them Sarah seemed able to forget her fears, but once she was deprived of their lively company, these returned, and deepened with the approach of night. She was able to swallow only a tiny portion of her dinner, and when the meal was over she retreated to a chair by the fire and sat huddled there, no longer making any pretence of joining in the conversation. She looked so small and forlorn that Justin was unexpectedly touched, and, taking the chair beside her, asked quietly how she was feeling.

"I do have the headache," she confessed in a low voice, adding apologetically: "I am sorry to be such poor company."

"And I am sorry to hear you say anything so absurd," he replied with a smile, "for under these circumstances it is foolish beyond permission. If I may make a suggestion, I think it would be a very good thing if you were to go to bed and endeavour to get a good night's sleep. You are quite worn out."

She agreed, but made no move to go, merely looking in an uncertain way at Chloe, engrossed in conversation with John on the other side of the fireplace. There was a brief pause, and then Justin said in a matter-of-fact way:

"Come, I will take you upstairs."

She cast him a grateful glance, allowed him to help her up from her chair and, bidding the others goodnight, went with him out of the room. The passage outside the coffee room was lit by an oil lamp which flickered eerily in the draught, and as they paused by the table where the bedroom candles were set out, Justin was not surprised to see Sarah glance nervously over her shoulder. He lit one of the candles, and then, as they went on along the passage, took her hand comfortingly in his. When they reached the cupboard by the foot of the stairs he felt her fingers tense in his clasp, but she said nothing until the door of her room was reached. Then she remarked in a tone of deep self-reproach:

"Thank you for coming with me. I never thought I could be so fainthearted, but pass that cupboard alone at night I could not."

"It would be quite surprising if you could," he replied, and reached past her to open the door. Beyond was darkness, broken only by the dull glow of the fire, and he went in with her, saying calmly as he began to light more candles: "Ring for your maid. I will wait until she comes."

She did so. He lit all the candles he could see, then stirred the fire so that the glowing logs blazed up and added yet more brightness, driving back the lurking shadows. Sarah drew a long breath of relief and smiled rather shakily at him.

"Thank you," she said again. "I am not usually so timorous, I assure you, but tonight—! Well, I am thankful that I shall not have to sleep alone in this room."

"I know." Justin came back to her where she still stood just inside the door. "It is natural that you should feel some uneasiness, but I am quite sure that there is no real cause for alarm." She nodded, but looked past him into the dimness of the passage, and after a moment he put out his hand to turn her face up towards him. "I mean that, Sarah," he said seriously. "In spite of what has happened, I am convinced that there is no danger to anyone else in this house. However, it may reassure you to know that my room is there, on the other side of the passage, and that I am not a heavy sleeper."

"It does reassure me."

Faint colour had come into her cheeks, but her

gaze met his steadily, and she did not try to move
away. For a long moment they looked at each other,
and then he bent his head and kissed her, but after
one instant of startled withdrawal, her lips grew
warmly responsive, so that the kiss became considerably more than the token of comfort and reassurance he had intended it to be. When he released
her, the colour was fairly flaming across her face
and she turned quickly away, pressing her hands to
her hot cheeks, while Justin, decidedly startled by
that swift, unexpected leap of feeling between them,
stood staring at her, for once completely at a loss.
Then he heard Lucy's hasty approaching footsteps,
and stepped quickly out into the passage.

"Your mistress has the headache and is going to
bed," he told the abigail, adding, under his breath:
"Don't leave her alone tonight, Lucy. She is still
more upset and frightened than she will admit."

"No wonder, the poor lamb, after what she went
through this morning," Lucy agreed in the same
tone. "You can trust me, my lord. I'll look after
her."

She went into the bedroom and closed the door,
and Justin went slowly, and very thoughtfully,
downstairs again.

It was some time before Chloe came up to bed,
but Sarah was not asleep. She tossed restlessly in the
shadows between the half-drawn curtains of the big
fourposter, and thought of Justin, and wondered
what impulse of kindness or compassion had
prompted him to kiss her, and burned with embarrassment at the memory of her own involuntary re-

sponse. What must he think of her, allowing her lips to cling so shamelessly to his? "Merely dutiful and submissive," Mama had said, and so she had meant to be, never allowing him to suspect the depth of her own feelings, but all her good resolutions had vanished at the first casual, careless intimacy. No wonder he had availed himself so promptly of the excuse to leave her afforded by Lucy's opportune arrival, not pausing even to bid her goodnight. He had forgiven the quite reprehensible conduct which had led to their present plight; had even, once he recovered his temper, appeared amused by it, so that it had seemed not beyond the bounds of possibility that they might eventually reach a comfortable understanding; but how could he forgive this? She had disregarded all Mama's warnings on how she must behave, and had no doubt disgusted him utterly.

When she heard Chloe come into the room she rolled over and buried her face in the pillow. Lucy, who while sitting by the fire, mending a tear which Tatters' sharp little teeth had made in the trimming of Sarah's gown, had cast several anxious glances towards the bed, got up as Miss Frensham entered, and said softly:

"Do you mind if I go downstairs for a minute or two, ma'am? I want to fetch Miss Sarah a dose of hartshorn and water, but his lordship said I was on no account to leave her alone." She lowered her voice still further. "She's still upset and frightened, he says, by what happened this morning."

"I don't wonder at it," Chloe agreed in the same

tone. "Go and fetch the hartshorn. I shall be with her now."

Lucy hurried away, and Chloe trod softly over to the bed, looked down at the dimly seen, huddled figure, and asked sympathetically:

"Is the headache very bad, Miss Lorymer? Would you like me to bathe your forehead?"

Sarah turned on to her back to look up at her. "You are very kind, but pray do not put yourself to that trouble. My head is not really too bad. It is just that—" She broke off and flung an arm across her eyes.

"Just that every time you start to fall asleep you recall what happened this morning," Chloe concluded, sympathetically but quite erroneously. "I'm not at all surprised, but you must not brood upon it, you know. I'm sure nothing else is going to happen."

"That is what Lord Chayle told me, and in any event, he says, his room is just across the passage and he is not a heavy sleeper."

"There you are, then! There's not the least need to be nervous," Chloe said in a rallying tone. "You have Lucy and me to keep you company, and I'll be bound his lordship will sleep with one eye open, as they say, to make sure nothing occurs to alarm you." She chuckled. "He's in quite a taking on your account—and so he should be, seeing that you are engaged to be married."

Sarah, feeling that some answer was required of her, said in a small voice that Lord Chayle had been very kind, and treated her tiresome fears with great forebearance.

"Forebearance?" Chloe repeated with the live-liest astonishment. "Upon my soul, that's an odd word for you to choose! I should look for a great deal more than forebearance, let me tell you, if I were in your shoes."

"You do not understand." Sarah spoke with dif-ficulty, swallowing a constriction in her throat. "Our engagement—it is not as you suppose. You must not think that there is any romantic attach-ment between us."

"Oh?" Chloe said sceptically. "Why mustn't I?"

"Because it is not true! We were scarcely ac-quainted when he offered for me, but it is his duty to marry—he has no heir—and he thought I would *suit*. That I would know how to conduct myself, and not be tiresome, or try to interfere." Sarah was becoming almost incoherent in her agitation, and very close to tears. "Oh, I should not be talking in this way! It is quite improper."

"Improper or not, it is plain you need to talk to someone," Chloe said bluntly, sitting down on the edge of the bed. "It's not only last night's ghastly business that is troubling you, is it?"

Sarah shook her head. Miss Frensham was clear-ly prepared to act as confidante, and though Sarah had a very clear idea of how Justin—or, for that matter, Mama—would regard any discussion of personal affairs with such a person as Chloe, she was in such miserable confusion that this seemed of little importance.

"I do not know what to do," she confessed unhappily. "I should never have agreed to marry him! Mama explained very carefully to me how it would be, and both she and Perry—my eldest brother—said they would not press me to accept any proposal repugnant to me, no matter what the advantages. Yet how could I refuse? We never dreamed that I would ever receive so splendid an offer, and I knew it was my duty to accept, for there are all my younger sisters to think of . . . " Her voice became wholly suspended by tears.

"Now let me understand this." Chloe, who had been listening with growing bewilderment, spoke in the tone of one determined to unravel a mystery. "You are not trying to make me believe, are you, that you don't want to marry Chayle?" Sarah hesitated, and after a moment Chloe added briskly: "Well, do you or don't you?"

"I do," Sarah whispered. "That is, I would if he felt even the smallest degree of—of fondness for me, but he does not. Indeed, how could he be expected to? I am not beautiful, like my sisters, or you, or—!"

"Or Mrs. Maitland," Chloe concluded as she hesitated. "I suppose there were any number of jealous gossipmongers eager to tell you about her? Though I'll gladly wager they didn't tell you that the affair is already over, which is what *I* have heard." She paused inquiringly, but when Sarah made no reply, added reassuringly: "Well, no doubt it all seems very shocking to an innocent like you, but you may take it from me that such affairs mean very little. Don't hold it against him."

"I don't," Sarah said in a stifled voice. "We did quarrel over her, but only because she was so insolent to me that it was past all bearing, and I slighted her in public. He was dreadfully angry."

"I dare say he was," Chloe agreed cheerfully, "for no man likes to be put in the wrong. Gave her a set-down, did you? I wish I might have been there to see it, for of all the——! However, that is neither here nor there. What did you mean when you said your Mama explained how it would be? About the Maitland woman?"

"Oh, no! It was my married cousin who told me of that, and warned me that a wife must pretend not to know or to care if her husband has a mistress, but it made me understand better what Mama meant."

"Meant by what?" Chloe demanded ruthlessly.

Sarah told her, faithfully recounting all Mama's admonitions and advice upon the behaviour expected of his wife by a man of Chayle's rank and breeding. Chloe listened with growing exasperation.

"Well, upon my word!" she said disgustedly at last. "I've no wish to seem disrespectful to your Mama, but I've never heard such a bag of moonshine in my life. All very well if one is marrying simply for the money and the title, not caring a snap of the fingers for the man himself, but you do care, don't you?"

"Yes," Sarah confessed with a sob, "I care far too much, and I am very much afraid that he has guessed it, and I feel ready to sink with mortification. I shall never be able to face him in the morning."

It required a good deal of encouragement to persuade her to be more explicit, but at length she was coaxed into telling enough for Chloe to form a reasonably accurate estimate of what had happened. If she thought it amusing, or a great deal of fuss over very little, she concealed this admirably, for she could see that Sarah was genuinely distressed; and no wonder, Chloe thought impatiently, when her fool of a mother had filled her head with so much high-flown prudery.

"Now you listen to me, Miss Lorymer," she said firmly. "Why Chayle offered for you, and how he regarded you then, does not matter in the least, for you say you were little more than strangers. Well, you are not strangers now, and I should be very much surprised to learn that he is as indifferent as you suppose. For one thing, it's plain that he thinks of you first and foremost, and the rest of us can go hang for all he cares. Why, he practically ordered me off to bed just now because, he said, you need to rest and he won't have you disturbed. As for walking off without saying goodnight—well, what else could he do, with Lucy coming along the passage? His lordship's a high stickler, and he wouldn't care to have a servant find him kissing you, even though you are engaged."

Lying back against the pillows, Sarah contemplated the novel idea that perhaps Mama was not infallible; that possibly her anxiety to spare her daughters the sort of disillusionment she herself had suffered had clouded her judgment; that Justin might not, after all, dislike the discovery that his future wife was in love with him.

"You really believe that?" she asked Chloe anxiously. "You are not just trying to be kind, because you found me in low spirits?"

"Much kindness there would be in telling you so if it weren't true."

"And you do not think he was shocked or repelled by the way I behaved?"

Chloe chuckled. "Quite the reverse, I should imagine, though he may have been a little surprised. Now that I come to think of it, he did look slightly bemused when he first came back to the parlour. No, my dear! If I know anything of men—and you may depend that I do, more, I dare say, than your Mama ever did or ever will—the only thing likely to repel him is if you try to freeze him to death with pretended indifference."

Sarah drew a deep breath and reached out to clasp Chloe's hand, gripping it hard. "Thank you," she said earnestly. "Thank you so very much. Oh, Miss Frensham, I am so glad I met you!"

"I suppose I had no business to talk to you as I have," Chloe said reflectively, "but you've treated me handsomely even though I know Chayle told you all about me. I couldn't stand by and see you make a mull of your whole future because of some antiquated notion that people of quality don't have feelings like ordinary men and women. Only never let him guess we had this talk, for he would have my blood if he knew!"

Chapter XI

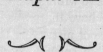

No alarms occurred to disturb them during the night, and in the morning, thanks to Chloe's worldly advice, Sarah was able to greet her betrothed with no more than a slightly heightened colour. He subjected her to a searching scrutiny, and nodded.

"Yes, you are looking much better this morning," he said with a smile. "I am very glad to see it, and also to be able to tell you that there have been no further falls of snow, and that there are even signs that a slight thaw may be beginning."

Chloe, who had accompanied Sarah downstairs, looked eagerly at him. "Does that mean we may soon be able to escape from this place? It cannot be too soon for me."

"Nor for any of us, I imagine," Justin replied. "It is too early to say, for the thaw will have to be a great deal more rapid than it is now before the road is open, and if it should freeze again later, conditions would be even worse than at present."

"And I suppose that with a rapid thaw there may be a danger of flooding," Sarah put in. "Oh dear, we may be marooned here for days yet."

"Oh, I think not," Justin replied encouragingly. "If the present improvement continues, I hope that by tomorrow one of the Ashlock boys will be able to get through to the village with news of what has happened here, and then, you may depend, we shall have constable and magistrate here as soon as it is humanly possible. Though, of course, none of us will be permitted to leave the inn until inquiries into the crime have been made."

Chloe stared. "You don't mean we shall all have to stay cooped up here until the murderer has been discovered?" she demanded. "Why, there's no knowing *how* long that may take!"

"Since the guilty person is obviously among those at present at the inn," Justin said dryly, "it is extremely unlikely that we shall all be permitted to disperse about our personal concerns until his identity has been made known." He saw that Sarah was looking profoundly dismayed, and added reassuringly: "Do not disturb yourself, my dear. As soon as you have described to the magistrate what happened yesterday, and answered any questions he may wish to put to you, I have every intention of removing you without delay to Lady Marlby's house."

"Will that be permitted?" she asked anxiously.

"Certainly it will." Justin spoke with a touch of hauteur, and she thought with a flash of amusement that it was unlikely any country magistrate would venture to dispute the matter with him. "It must be obvious even to the meanest intelligence that *you* have nothing to hide, and though I am prepared for you to remain for the present in this neighbourhood, you will do so in more fitting surroundings than these."

Chloe had moved away from them to stand staring from the window, frowning, and drumming her fingers impatiently on the sill; obviously she did not relish the prospect of yet further delays. Sarah looked up at Justin.

"Will you stay with me at Grandmama's, my lord?" she asked in a low voice.

"That rather depends upon her ladyship," he countered. "I fear she holds me in aversion, and you told me yourself that she dislikes our betrothal."

"Only, I am sure, because she is not much acquainted with you," Sarah told him earnestly. "When she knows you better, she will realize that she has been mistaken."

"Will she?" His eyes were warm with amusement, and something more. "Such certainty on your part, my dear Sarah, encourages me to hope that *you* have undergone a similar change of heart."

She flushed, but recalled Chloe's advice and did not try to dissemble, saying rather shyly: "I had no need to, sir, except when I was so very angry with you. As for Grandmama, I am very deeply attached to her, and I think she is fond of me, and I wish very much for our betrothal to have her approval.

She has a sharp tongue, and Perry and the others are all a little afraid of her, but she has never shown *me* anything but the greatest kindness."

"You terrify me, ma'am," he said solemnly. "Perhaps we should defy the officers of the law, and go back to London instead. Or may I depend upon you to protect me from her ladyship?"

This drew a chuckle from her, but before she could reply, John Roman walked into the parlour. He looked pale and haggard, as though he had not slept well, and when he had bidden them good morning, said abruptly to Justin:

"That fellow Layton is out in the stables again. I went to cast an eye over my horse, and there he was, questioning Clem Ashlock very closely about the state of the roads, and whether they are likely to be open first towards Dover or towards London. You know, there's no denying his behaviour is dashed suspicious."

"I do not agree, Mr. Roman," Sarah said sharply. "If Mr. Layton *were* guilty of this dreadful crime, surely he would be doing everything in his power to avert suspicion and not drawing attention upon himself in this way?"

"And we must bear in mind," Justin pointed out, "that Layton was just as anxious to go on his way *before* Bodicote's death. I will admit I think him unwise to be so secretive about the purpose of his journey, but perhaps he will speak more freely to the magistrate when he comes. If his business in Dover is of a very private nature there is no reason in the world why he should disclose it to us. Or, indeed, any reason why we should inquire into it." He turned to Sarah, drawing a chair out from the table for her. "Will you be seated, Miss Lorymer? They will be bringing breakfast directly."

It was very plain that the subject, as far as he was concerned, was now closed. John flushed and bit his lip, clearly put out by this courteous rebuff, but before he could say anything, Chloe came to join Sarah at table, remarking brightly that she was quite sharp-set, and maintaining a flow of small talk during the two or three minutes which passed before Polly and Eliza came in with laden trays.

Sarah noticed that John was unusually silent throughout the meal, and hoped that he would soon come out of the sullens. They were all under a strain, and if he was going to take offence for so slight a cause, and show it so clearly, she could place no dependence upon Justin's continuing good humour. If they began to quarrel among themselves, she thought anxiously, a difficult situation would soon become intolerable.

To her relief, Mr. Roman excused himself as soon as the meal was over, and presently, when Polly was clearing the table, Sarah caught a glimpse of him, through the open door, in earnest conversation with Mr. Chebworth by the coffee-room fire. She had been thinking of her own conversation with Justin before breakfast, and when Polly had gone back to the kitchen, she remarked with a frown:

"You know, I do not see how questioning the people here will reveal the identity of the murderer. I realize, of course, that the guilty person *must* be among those at present at the inn, but he is not likely, is he, to offer any information which will incriminate him, and nobody else seems to know anything at all about what happened."

"That's true," Chloe agreed. "I've been thinking along the same lines myself, and it appears to me that we are likely to be kept kicking our heels here for a long time. Why, we do not even know anything about the poor fellow who was murdered, except his name, and the fact that he boarded the coach in London, bound for Canterbury."

"I suppose," Sarah said reflectively, "that when he does not return home, his family will make inquiries, but for all we know, he may have been expected to stay away for some time, in which case he will not immediately be missed." She turned to Justin. "My lord, what do you imagine the magistrate will do? Will he call in the Bow Street Runners?"

"I have not the smallest idea." Justin, who felt that any speculation which coupled Mr. Bodicote with Bow Street was best avoided, spoke with studied indifference. "Happily, this is not a decision which we shall be called upon to make, so there is no need for us to vex our minds over it. No doubt the magistrate will take whatever measures he feels to be necessary."

He saw that his reply had not found favour with either lady. Sarah's big brown eyes regarded him reproachfully, and Chloe said, with a hard little laugh:

"But Lord Chayle does not intend to bother himself over the question. To be sure, it was excessively tiresome of Bodicote to get himself murdered under the same roof as your lordship, was it not?"

"The whole situation is excessively tiresome," he retorted blightingly, making the most of this opportunity to discourage speculation. "A more unsavoury business it has never been my misfortune to encounter, and it is likely to become more so, I fear, before the mystery is resolved." He saw the sudden uneasiness in her eyes and smiled faintly, without amusement. "Precisely, my dear Chloe! Bodicote was not killed without reason, and though Layton may appear to be a convenient scapegoat, I fear we cannot expect the authorities to accept him as the murderer without inquiring very closely into the affairs of everyone present in this house when the crime was committed. An intrusion the prospect of which is as distasteful to me as I am persuaded it must be to you."

She looked at him very hard, as though suspecting him of some hidden meaning, but she had sufficient experience as an actress to be able to disguise her true feelings, and merely said with a shrug:

"Well, it is not very pleasant to have strangers prying into one's private concerns, no matter how innocent these may be. To my mind, Layton's own conduct makes him the only possible suspect, but that is merely my personal opinion."

Sarah thought this somewhat arbitrary, and wondered why Chloe should be so eager to pin the guilt for the crime on to the hapless Mr. Layton, but that others might be equally eager she did not suspect until later that day. Then, finding Toby alone in the coffee room with Tatters, she paused to inquire how the training of the pup was progressing. As soon as the little dog saw her, however, it came prancing across to greet her, and Toby, after several fruitless attempts to call it to order, abandoned the attempt and instead remarked conversationally:

"Miss Lorymer, ma'am, do *you* think as Mr. Layton done it?"

Sarah, who had been stooping to fondle the puppy, straightened up abruptly, looking startled.

"Did what, Toby?"

"Murdered Mr. Bodicote," the boy replied. "They're saying in there," he jerked his head towards the taproom, "that o' course he done it and ought to be put under lock and key till the constable comes to fetch him away. The coachman said we might all be murdered in our beds if Mr. Layton was let to roam about loose, and Mrs. Joe heard him and swooned clean away. Then Mr. Badsey reminded the coachman as his lordship had warned him once to keep his mouth shut, and that if he didn't, *he'd* shut it for him."

"Toby, it is most improper for you to talk in this way," Sarah said severely. "There is not the smallest reason to suppose Mr. Layton guilty of this dreadful crime, and it is quite wrong—indeed, wicked—to make unfounded accusations of that kind. What, pray, would your uncle say if he knew that you were repeating such ignorant, malicious gossip?"

"He couldn't say nothing, ma'am," Toby replied sulkily, " 'cause he believes it, too. I heard him say so to Joe Ashlock."

Sarah was dismayed. Wild talk in the taproom was one thing, and, under the circumstances, only to be expected, but Mr. Chebworth had impressed her as a man of solid common sense; slow thinking, perhaps, but not the sort of person to be carried away by specious arguments across the alepots.

"They say," Toby pursued, seeing that he now had her whole attention, "that likely Mr. Layton and Mr. Bodicote knew each other all along, although they pretended not to. Up to no good, the coachman says they must have been, else why was Mr. Layton in such a fret, and why is he so anxious to be off to Dover afore anyone can come after him from London? P'raps they'd stolen something very valuable, and quarrelled over it, and that's why he killed Mr. Bodicote."

"Toby, that is quite enough!" Sarah broke in sternly. "I have never heard a wilder flight of fancy in my life, and if that is the sort of nonsense they are talking in the taproom, the less you listen to it, the better. *I* certainly wish to hear no more of it." A thought struck her. "Where *is* Mr. Layton? I do not recall seeing him today."

"Skulking in his room," Toby replied with relish, obviously repeating a phrase he had overheard. "He's been there nearly all day—aye, and he'd better stay there, the coachman says, if he knows what's good for him."

With this parting shot he tucked Tatters under his arm and stalked out of the room, clearly much offended by her reception of his information. Sarah remained where she was, frowning at the somewhat

motheaten fox-mask which adorned the wall above
the fireplace, and trying to convince herself that the
uneasiness aroused by Toby's disclosures was
without foundation. She had been as much frightened as shocked by what he had told her, for there
seemed to her to be something almost sinister in the
way so many occupants of the inn were convincing
themselves of Layton's guilt. Confined as they were
to the house, with nothing to do but drink and talk,
such conviction, she thought, might very easily become dangerous unless something were done to
check it.

She wondered whether she ought to tell Justin
what she had learned, but was restrained from
doing so by a doubt which had lingered uncomfortably at the back of her mind all day; a doubt inspired by his attitude that morning when she and
Chloe had been speaking of the murder. He had
seemed indifferent, almost bored, and Sarah had
been wondering ever since whether Chloe's gibe that
he found the whole tragedy merely tiresome could
possibly be justified.

Only one alternative occurred to her, and she hesitated to put that into practice because it seemed
to her a bold, almost improper thing to do. For a
few minutes she struggled with her qualms, then,
deciding that purity of motive must be sufficient excuse, went determinedly out of the coffee room and
up the stairs.

The bedchambers of the Rose in Hand were not
so many in number that she had difficulty in finding

the one she sought. Justin's, as he had told her, was directly opposite to her own, and she knew that the one beyond it, on the corner of the building, was John Roman's, because he had complained, during their first day at the inn, of the way in which its windows had caught the full violence of the storm. Beyond that the passage again turned at a sharp right angle towards the back of the house, and since it was to be supposed that the Ashlock family would have its quarters over the kitchen, the rooms nearer to the front must be the lesser chambers for the use of guests.

Sarah tapped timidly on the first of the closed doors, resisted an impulse to take flight when she heard movement within, and then the door opened and she braced herself to meet Mr. Layton's astonished and suspicious gaze. Before he could say anything she hurried into low-voiced, breathless speech.

"You will think it odd in me, I know, to come seeking you like this, but I feel it only right to warn you of the degree of suspicion your conduct has aroused. They are saying in the taproom that you must be guilty, and are making all manner of wild guesses to account for your refusal to disclose the purpose of your journey. It is no concern of mine, I know, but for your own sake, Mr. Layton, will you not consider the wisdom of using a little frankness?"

He continued to stare rather owlishly down at her, swaying a little even though he was holding onto the door with one hand and the doorpost with the other; he said in a thickened voice: "Private business. Private and personal. Don't concern anyone here."

She realized that he had been drinking again, and suspected that her warning was falling on deaf ears, but that indefinable uneasiness urged her to persist. She said, still softly but with decided sharpness:

"Mr. Layton, a murder has been committed. None of us will be permitted to leave this place without giving satisfactory answers to the magistrate, so do you not see how foolish it is to persist in such secrecy? You are simply making matters worse for yourself."

"Don't know anything about it," he insisted with drunken obstinacy. "Don't remember what happened that night. My business in Dover's nothing to do with you. Nothing to do with anyone here. Go away, an' leave me alone."

He retreated without giving her a chance to reply, and Sarah was left staring at the outside of a closed door. She hesitated, half raising her hand to knock again but realizing in time the futility of it. Layton was in no state to listen to advice or warning; the purpose of his journey, whatever it was, appeared to possess his mind to the exclusion of everything else, even the murder, and he seemed incapable of appreciating the gravity of his situation. She was wasting her time and had better return to the parlour before she was found out in an act which would certainly displease Chayle if he learned of it.

She turned away, and had just rounded the corner of the passage when she heard a light footstep mounting the stairs. She gasped, and whisked back out of sight, catching a fleeting glimpse of Chloe's blue gown at the far end of the corridor as she did so. Flattening herself against the wall, she waited with pounding heart, hoping that she had not been seen, for though her movements were nothing to do with Miss Frensham, she had no wish to provoke curiosity or comment.

After a minute or so she ventured to peep round the corner, and saw with relief that the passage was empty. Chloe must have gone into their room without noticing her. She stole forward, and was level with John Roman's room before she realized that it was this one, and not their own, which Chloe had entered, for the door, imperfectly fastened, had swung partly open to reveal, within, Chloe and John locked in each other's arms and totally unaware that they were being observed. For one shocked and fascinated instant Sarah stared at them, then fled past on tiptoe and into the sanctuary of the big bedchamber.

She felt hot with embarrassment at the implications of what she had seen. Like any well-brought-up young girl of her day she had led a rigorously sheltered life, and though she knew in theory what Justin meant when he described Chloe Frensham as one of "the muslin company," the knowledge had made no real impact upon her until her glimpse of that passionate embrace. Though this had been wholly accidental, she felt as shamed by it as though she had been deliberately prying; yet more shaming still was the thought which now forced itself into her mind—the thought that she would like Justin to kiss her in the way John had been kissing Chloe.

It was some time before she could compose herself sufficiently to go downstairs again, and into the presence of her betrothed. She found him in the coffee room, discussing with Mr. Chebworth the change in the weather, and the chances of soon being able to summon help. These now seemed reasonably good, for the wind had veered round to the south, the air was noticeably milder, and there was every promise of the thaw continuing.

When they retired that night, it was to the sound of the drip and trickle of melting snow, and Sarah's last waking thought was a thankful one that the adventure was nearing its end. The uneasiness which had prompted her warning to Layton had not diminished; she felt awkward now in the presence of Chloe and John; and Justin's attitude of bored indifference towards the murder lingered disturbingly in her mind. Surely he could not be as callous as his remarks seemed to indicate?

She passed a restless night, and was startled into sudden wakefulness by the sound of raised voices and hurrying footsteps somewhere below. She started up on to one elbow, aware that beside her in the curtained darkness of the big bed Chloe, too, had roused in alarm and was saying, in a voice still drugged with sleep:

"What is it? What's happening?"

Sarah reached out and fumbled to part the bed-curtains. It was still dark, but the fire, which had been banked high when they went to bed, had sunk to a small heap of dully glowing embers, so the night must be well advanced. Out of the dimness came Lucy's frightened whisper.

"Oh, Miss Sarah, something's wrong! Listen to the to-do downstairs."

Shivering, Sarah slipped out of bed, groped for dressing gown and slippers, and stumbled across to the fireplace, where she succeeded in kindling a taper and then a candle. In its feeble light she and her two companions looked at one another with fearful speculation, hearing footsteps and voices nearer at hand now, in the passage leading to the stairs.

Sarah went across to the door and stood there listening, straining her ears to catch some hint of the cause of the commotion. Several minutes passed, during which Chloe got out of bed and, lacking a dressing gown, helped herself to Lucy's thick cloak from the cupboard. Lucy herself was still huddled in the trestle-bed, with only her frightened face visible above the blankets. Presently, seeing Sarah put her hand to the latch of the door, she was moved to apprehensive protest.

"Miss Sarah, don't you leave this room! For all we know, that murdering villain might be just outside."

"Nonsense!" Sarah replied as firmly as chattering teeth would allow. "We must find out what has happened. Besides, I can hear Lord Chayle's voice, and there can be no danger to us if he is there."

She opened the door a few inches and looked out, just as his lordship appeared from the direction of the stairs. He wore a rather splendid brocaded dressing gown, and his fair hair was ruffled, but Sarah was too greatly concerned to be embarrassed either by the informality of his attire or her own.

"Don't be alarmed," he said as soon as he saw her. "I was just coming to reassure you, for I guessed you must have been awakened by the noise." He saw the anxiety in her face, and added in a matter-of-fact tone: "Layton has just been discovered in the stable, trying to make off with one of the horses."

"I knew it!" Chloe, peering over Sarah's shoulder, spoke triumphantly. "That proves he's guilty. He knew the constable would be sent for now the thaw's set in, and he decided to make a run for it."

"It proves nothing, ma'am, but the extent of Layton's folly," Justin replied curtly. "In weather like this, and being unfamiliar with the country, he would most certainly have lost his way."

"What will happen now?" Sarah asked in a low voice.

"He will be taken back to his room and confined there until the magistrate arrives. That will be best for all concerned." Justin had been frowning, but his stern expression relaxed as he looked down at her, and he added more gently: "You are shivering, my dear. Go back to bed, for it is not yet six o'clock."

She hesitated, but the sound of footsteps and voices on the stairs indicated that others, presumably Mr. Layton and his captors, were approaching, and she had no wish to see or be seen by them. She drew back into the room, obliging Chloe to do the same, and quietly closed the door.

Chapter XII

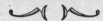

It soon became apparent that Chayle's moderate view of Mr. Layton's attempted flight was not shared by the rest of the company, who were wholly at one with Chloe in regarding it as incontestable proof of his guilt. Sarah discovered, to her dismay, that everyone now seemed to regard the mystery as solved, and looked on the expected coming of constable and magistrate merely as a tiresome formality to be gone through before they were all allowed to go their various ways. Layton's frantic protests of innocence were disregarded, and from the attitude of the rougher element present Sarah concluded that Justin's decision to confine him to his room had been made as much for the man's own protection as anything else.

Chayle himself had made no further comment on the matter, and she was still half inclined to believe him indifferent to the outcome and as anxious as ev-

eryone else for a scapegoat to be found. Deeply
troubled by the thought, she brooded over it until,
midway through the morning, he joined her and
Chloe in the parlour and told them that Joe Ashlock
had set out for the village.

"Not on foot, surely?" Sarah asked in a shocked
tone.

"No, he has his own horse, a sturdy beast well
accustomed to the road. The nearest magistrate is a
Mr. Melchett, whose house lies close to the village,
and Ashlock will go on there with the constable. I
have given him a letter to carry to Melchett, telling
him what has happened."

"When do you suppose the magistrate will
come?" Chloe asked. "Today?"

"It is possible, but much depends on the time it
takes Ashlock to reach the village, and what sort of
conditions he encounters. Melchett will perceive the
need for haste, but may consider it prudent to delay
his visit until tomorrow."

"Well, it's to be hoped he comes at once," Chloe
said shortly. "*I* shall feel happier when Layton has
been taken off to gaol, and I dare say all the other
women feel the same."

Sarah frowned. "I should, Miss Frensham, if
there were any real proof that Mr. Layton is the
murderer, but I cannot see that there is. The fact
that he tried to leave the inn does not necessarily
mean that he is guilty."

"What else can it mean?" Chloe retorted irritably. "Do you suppose he was simply in a hurry to
get to Dover? Besides, it was only he and Bodicote

who took pains not to let fall any scrap of information about themselves, so you may be sure they both had something to hide. Something they quarrelled over."

"I wondered when we should come to that," Justin remarked ironically. "Where such a supposition originated I cannot imagine, unless it were with young Toby. I hope it was. A *boy's* high flights may be forgiven."

"Oh, you may laugh, my lord, but let me tell you that I am not the only one who thinks so! And I'll wager this Mr. Melchett will think the same. After all, what could be more likely?"

"Almost anything, I should imagine," Justin replied witheringly. "Layton is under suspicion, certainly, as we all are, and has not helped himself by his conduct, but Miss Lorymer is right in saying that there is no real proof of his guilt. Under the circumstances it is natural—though by no means admirable—for those involved to seek a scapegoat, but let me assure you, as I am prepared to assure the rest of the company, that I have no intention of permitting a possibly innocent man to become the victim of a witch-hunt."

There was an angry colour in Chloe's cheeks, and a hard, unpleasant look about her mouth. She said viciously: "You are so convinced of his innocence, my lord, that one wonders whether you know more than you have admitted about the affair."

Sarah uttered a gasp of indignation and turned involuntarily to Justin. He was looking at Chloe, not angrily, as might have been expected, but with an icy contempt which darkened the colour in her cheeks yet, at the same time, brought a trace of uneasiness into her expression. She rose to her feet and faced him defiantly, obviously regretting what she had said but too stubborn to retract it.

"And you are so convinced of his guilt," Justin said coldly, "that one is tempted to wonder the same about you."

For a second or two Chloe continued to face him, but the disdain in his eyes was more than even her assurance could withstand. She tossed her head and flounced out of the room, shutting the door behind her with a decided slam. Sarah said uneasily:

"You do not really believe that, do you?"

He turned to her, the impatient frown with which he had watched Chloe's departure fading from his face. "Do you suppose I would permit her to continue to share your room if I did? Miss Frensham grows impertinent, and will be the better for a setdown."

"And you do not think it of Mr. Layton, either?"

"My dear Sarah, I simply do not know, but I will not allow him to be tried and condemned even before any proper inquiry into the crime has been made. He is an exceedingly foolish fellow, and his attempted flight this morning was as ill-judged an action as one can imagine, but he has as much right to justice as any of us."

"I think," Sarah confessed reluctantly, in a small, guilty voice, "that *I* may have had something to do with what happened this morning. You see, I warned him yesterday of the growing suspicion of him and tried to persuade him to use a little more frankness." She saw the look of astonishment and, she thought, displeasure, in his lordship's eyes, and hurried into an account of her conversation with Toby, adding, when she reached the end of it: "I know that children are apt to exaggerate, but I did not think that Toby would tell me an outright lie, and when he said that even his uncle had come to believe Mr. Layton guilty, I felt I had to do *something*. To see one of our number singled out by so much suspicion and ill feeling seemed—oh, *sinister*, somehow! Even—though this you will think absurd —dangerous."

"I do not think it absurd. In circumstances such as these, with everyone's nerves on the stretch, an unpleasant situation could very easily develop. It came close to doing so this morning. I could wish, though, that you had come to me with your misgivings." He paused, looking at her rather hard. "Why did you not?"

She coloured, and fidgeted with the fringe of the silk shawl draped about her shoulders. "I thought of doing so," she admitted hesitantly, "but—forgive me—it seemed to me that you were not particularly interested. I know now that I was mistaken, and I beg your pardon, but every time one of us began to speculate upon the identity of the murderer, you immediately turned the conversation as though this were of no account and began instead to talk of something quite trivial. As though, as Miss Frensham said, you found the whole matter merely tiresome."

"I see," Justin said in a curious tone. "I have mismanaged everything, it seems."

"No!" Something in his voice brought Sarah quickly to his side, her hand on his arm. "I misunderstood, that is all." She paused, her gaze earnestly searching his face. "Justin, what is it? Why will you not trust me?"

"Not trust you?" he repeated in astonishment, laying his hand over hers. "My dear child—!"

"No," she interrupted quietly, "I am not a child. I am twenty years old and soon to become your wife. I know I behaved foolishly in running away as I did, but that does not mean that I am entirely without common sense."

"No, only when you lose your temper," he replied with a fleeting smile, then paused, studying her now as gravely as she had studied him—as she continued to do, her gaze meeting his steadily, without reserve. After a moment or two he gave an odd little laugh, and his fingers tightened upon hers. "But I believe we are making an end of misunderstanding between us, Sarah, are we not?"

"I hope so," she whispered. "Oh, Justin, I hope it so very much."

He lifted her hand from his arm but continued to hold it, rubbing his thumb gently to and fro across the back of it. After a moment he said in a low voice: "Bodicote was a Bow Street Runner. He told me so, in confidence, only a few hours before he was killed."

Sarah's eyes widened enormously; her lips parted. At first she was too astonished to speak, and then she said in a whisper: "But why did nobody find out—afterwards? Should a Runner not carry some proof of his authority?" Then, answering her own question: "The murderer knew, and destroyed the proof?"

"I imagine so. He would suppose, you see, that no one else at the inn was aware of Bodicote's profession, and would therefore account the secret safe. It appeared to me better for all concerned to discourage any speculation until the facts can be laid before a magistrate."

"And I thought you merely bored and disgusted with the whole dreadful affair," Sarah said in a tone of deep self-reproach. "Justin, forgive me."

He smiled. "For what? I am aware that I must have appeared disgracefully indifferent to the poor fellow's fate, but situated as we are, stranded here with an undoubted murderer among us, it seemed to me that my first concern must be to protect those who were unquestionably innocent. You, Sarah. The other women, and that infernally inquiring youngster. A man who has killed once may kill again if he fancies himself in danger of discovery." Sarah gave an involuntary shiver, and he added ruefully: "I should not have allowed you to cajole me into telling you this. We are not out of the wood yet."

"I will be very careful," she promised, "and not breathe a word of it to anyone." She looked at him with a puzzled frown. "But why was he here? Was he in pursuit of a criminal?"

"He was endeavouring to catch a thief, but the

immediate reason for his presence aboard that
stagecoach was the fact that Chloe Frensham was
also among the passengers." He smiled at the expression on Sarah's face. "Come, sit down again
and I will tell you as much as I know, though I
warn you that it still makes no sense of what followed."

Leading her back to the chairs by the fire, he sat
down with her and recounted the story of the silver
music-box, as Mr. Bodicote had told it to him.

"It is ludicrous, is it not?" he concluded. "I
imagine that it is a case of family spite, as Bodicote
said. No doubt the young man felt himself very
hardly used when his uncle had the impertinence to
marry and father a son, thus depriving him of his
expectations."

"Yes, I suppose so," Sarah replied slowly. "Justin, what if Mr. Roman were Christopher Frome?"

He looked astonished. "My dear, how could he
be? He could not have foreseen that Chloe Frensham would be stranded here. Her intended destination was Canterbury, and Frome will be expecting to meet her there."

"Yes, I know, but he, too, could have been
stranded here by chance. He told me that he had
come from the direction of Clitterbury, and the
shortest way from there to Canterbury is a lane
which joins this road a mile or so back. Only if one
is travelling post, and needs to hire a fresh team, is
it necessary to go by way of the village. Mr. Roman
is riding, is he not?"

"Yes, but if he and Chloe Frensham are both

—

here by chance, they would have been taken by surprise when they met, and would certainly have betrayed themselves."

"No, for he was in the coffee room when she was carried through unconscious, but I did not see him there when I took her up to bed. He could have discovered in which room she was lodged, and disclosed his presence to her while you and I were dining, and Lucy was in the kitchen."

"Warning her that, since we were all snowbound here, it would be safer to behave as though they were strangers?" Justin considered the suggestion, but then shook his head. "It is an ingenious theory, Sarah, but do not take it amiss when I say that there is not the smallest reason for supposing it to be true."

"There is one thing," she said, blushing a little. "She visited Mr. Roman in his room yesterday." She hesitated, decided that she could not bring herself to describe to Chayle exactly what she had seen, and went on: "I saw her go in—though she does not know that, of course—and I suspect it was not for the first time." He did not reply, and she added accusingly: "I suppose you think that proves nothing, either?"

"I think," he said with some amusement, "that this is a highly improper subject for us to be discussing at all. And before you rip up at me, my love, allow me to point out that even if your theory is correct, it sheds no light at all upon the identity of poor Bodicote's murderer. A man does not kill over so trifling a matter as the theft of a music-box, espe-

cially as it seems extremely unlikely that the elder
Mr. Frome will allow his family name to be dragged
through the courts for so slight a reason. I imagine
that his only purpose is to recover his property and
give his nephew a severe fright."

Sarah was too disconcerted by the lightly spoken
endearment he had used to resent his indulgent dis-
missal of her suggestion. She directed a startled,
questioning glance towards him, and found that he
was watching her with an expression in his grey eyes
which made her heart beat faster, and strengthened
her growing conviction that Chloe had been right
and Mama wrong. She felt her cheeks grow hotter
still, and in a vain attempt to dissemble her confusion, said hurriedly:

"I expect you are right, but then *who* could have
committed the crime, and why?"

He continued to watch her, smiling, but answered the question gravely enough. "I can only
surmise that there is some criminal among our
number whom Bodicote belatedly recognized and
was foolish enough to challenge. With all respect to
the poor fellow, he did not give me the impression
of being particularly adept as an officer of the law,
nor is it likely that a truly expert thief-taker would
have been assigned to so trivial a matter as Mr.
Frome's music-box."

"No, I suppose not," she agreed reluctantly. "Oh,
poor Mr. Bodicote! He seemed such a kindly man,
and he was getting old, and perhaps he had never
been very good at catching criminals." Her voice
trembled suddenly and she jumped up from her

chair. "Justin, I shall be so *thankful* to leave this horrid little inn!"

"I know." He got up and came to her side. "And I shall be more than thankful to have you safely away from it. We did not bargain for this, did we, when first we found ourselves stranded here?"

"I am being tiresome," Sarah said unsteadily, "and all because of a mere irritation of the nerves, which is something I have no patience with. Pay no heed to me!"

"What an infamous thing it would be if I did not," he said with a smile. "You have every reason to be overwrought, but keep up your spirits with the thought that it cannot now be long before I am able to place you in Lady Marlby's care."

"I have been thinking about that, too," Sarah admitted ruefully, "and it occurs to me that Grandmama will give me a tremendous scold for allowing myself to become involved in anything as vulgar as a murder. There is no denying that she is a trifle straitlaced in her notions."

"Possibly she is." There was the faintest tremor of laughter in Justin's voice. "She can scarcely blame you, however, for something which is in no way your fault."

Sarah sighed. "But it *is* my fault. If I had not run away from London, neither you nor I would ever have put up at the Rose in Hand."

"If you had not run away, we would still be strangers to each other," he pointed out. "Is not our better understanding worth a scold? And you will not be obliged to face it alone, you know. I shall be with you to take my share of the blame, which, from what you have told me of her ladyship's opinion of me, will no doubt be the larger. In fact, I shall not be at all surprised if she blames *me* for allowing you to become involved in this unsavoury affair."

That made Sarah laugh. "Oh no, how could she, when you are here entirely on my account? I said that she is straitlaced, sir, not unjust."

"Ah, but it was I who provoked you into running away, remember, and though I came after you, my motive, I must confess, was by no means altogether praiseworthy. I was anxious, certainly, but concern came a very long way behind annoyance."

"I know." She glanced mischievously up at him. "Indeed, I cannot think why I should be in a quake over the scolding I may get from Grandmama, after the one I received from you."

"Which you richly deserved," he retorted. "And do not try to tell me, ma'am, that you were in a quake then, because I shall not believe you."

"Oh no," she said candidly. "I was too angry, you see, and had been from the time you took me home from Lady Bellingham's party. It is odd, is it not, that the moment I lost my temper with you, I stopped being afraid of you?"

"Afraid of me?" he repeated in a stunned voice. "Good God! You were never that, surely?"

"Of course I was—well, in awe of you, at least! You seemed so unapproachable. You had never paid me the least attention beyond the demands of ordinary civility, and there seemed no reason in the world why you should ask me to marry you. I have

neither beauty nor fortune, and though Mama said
you wanted a quiet, comfortable wife who would
not make herself tiresome, I still could not understand why you should have chosen me." She hesitated, and then added rather wistfully: "I still do not
know."

Justin, casting his mind back with some difficulty
to the moment when he had decided to offer for
Sarah Lorymer, was ashamed to recall that he had
done so largely out of perversity. This seemed incredible to him now, and he knew that it was something which Sarah herself must never be allowed to
suspect.

"At the time I proposed to you," he said quietly,
"your Mama's estimate of my reasons for doing so
was very largely correct, and I suppose that is why I
was infuriated by the incident at Lady Bellingham's. My quiet, conformable bride-to-be was behaving entirely out of character, and being very tiresome indeed. I found I had to make her acquaintance all over again." He looked down at her anxious, upturned face, and with his forefinger gently
traced the line of her cheek. "Do you know, I like
the second Miss Lorymer so very much better than
the first?"

Her swift colour rose beneath his touch, but she
said in a rallying tone, albeit somewhat breathlessly:
"But you were still very angry with her."

"I was," he admitted, "and something tells me
that there will be times in the future when I shall be
just as angry with her again. Do you imagine that

we can spend the rest of our lives together without quarrelling now and then?"

"Well, no," she agreed cautiously, "but I promise that I will not let you provoke me into doing anything outrageous."

He laughed, and caught her in his arms. "Sarah, Sarah, do not make rash promises you will not be able to keep! When you lose your temper you will never pause to think until it is too late, and well you know it."

He looked down at her, still laughing, and then abruptly his expression sobered again. He held her more closely and bent his head, and Sarah, recklessly casting to the wind all Mama's precepts, clung tightly to him and responded eagerly to his kisses. Far from being repelled by this betrayal of feeling, his lordship appeared to derive great satisfaction from it, and continued to cradle her in his arms, murmuring some very gratifying endearments, until the sound of voices and movement in the coffee room reminded them that their present privacy might be invaded at any moment. He then let her go with every evidence of reluctance, and Sarah, quite dazed with happiness, had a chance to spare a grateful thought for Chloe, whose advice was now proved, to Sarah's satisfaction at least, to be a great deal better than Mama's.

Chapter XIII

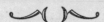

The magistrate did not come to the Rose in Hand that day. Joe Ashlock, returning to the inn just as darkness was falling, informed them that as Mr. Melchett expected his inquiries to take some time, he proposed to set out with the constable at first light, and hoped to be with them at a reasonably early hour.

"Which I reckon he will do, my lord," Joe concluded, "It be thawing fast now, and from what I could see of it, though there's a lot of slush and water about, the pike-road should be open by morning. We've been lucky this time, the wind veering round to the west like it has."

Justin agreed, and Joe, having handed over Mr. Melchett's reply to his lordship's letter, went off to the kitchen. With a word of excuse to Sarah and John Roman, who were with him in the parlour, Justin broke the seal and glanced quickly through the letter; then, finding the gaze of both his companions fixed expectantly upon him, shook his head with a slight smile.

"Melchett expresses his shocked dismay at the news I sent, and assures me that he will do all in his power to assist us. That is all."

He did not feel it necessary to add that, from the obsequious tone of the letter, it seemed that Mr. Melchett was one of those who set undue importance upon a title. This was a fact which might prove to have both advantages and disadvantages, the former being that he was unlikely to place any obstacle in the way of his lordship removing Miss Lorymer from the inn at the earliest opportunity, and the latter that it was only too probable that he would try to defer to Chayle's opinion on every other matter as well.

Chloe came into the parlour and the news was passed on to her, but though she expressed her satisfaction, and the hope that they would soon be allowed to go their separate ways, it occurred to Sarah that she looked as though something had vexed her. Since tempers in general were tending by this time to become a little frayed, she thought no more about this until she went upstairs just before dinner and found her abigail bearing unmistakable signs of having recently been crying.

"Lucy!" Sarah exclaimed in dismay. "Whatever is the matter?"

"Nothing, miss," Lucy replied, sniffing. "I think I've just taken a bit of a cold, that's all."

"Nonsense!" Sarah said briskly. "You have been

crying, and I want to know why." She watched with
mild exasperation the stubborn pressing together of
her maid's lips, and added bluntly: "You may as
well tell me first as last, for you know very well that
I will have the truth in the end."

Lucy admitted this with a watery smile, and after
another brief hesitation said with a rush:

"It's that Miss Frensham, miss! I'd be grateful if
you'd tell her I'm not in the habit of poking and prying into what don't concern me, nor yet of pilfering
from any lady I'm attending on, be she what she
may."

Sarah stared at her in astonishment. "I am sure
there is not the least need for me to tell Miss Frensham anything of the sort. Do you mean she has accused you of such a thing?

Lucy sniffed again. "As good as, miss. I was up
here earlier on, setting some of your things to rights,
when I saw that little silver vinaigrette she uses lying
on the floor under the dressing table. I remembered
seeing Miss Frensham's reticule hanging in the cupboard, under her pelisse, and I thought I'd just
drop the vinaigrette in there so it wouldn't get mis-
laid again. I'd just got the bag in my hands when
she walked in, and set up such a screech it's a
wonder you didn't all hear it and think someone
else was being murdered. Swore at me, she did, and
dared me ever to lay a finger on anything of hers
again."

Sarah was frowning. "I thought she looked vexed
when she came into the parlour, but what in the
world made her behave in such an odd fashion? She

cannot seriously have supposed that you were going through her reticule." She saw that Lucy was still torn between distress and anger, and decided that it was more important to soothe the abigail's ruffled feelings than to search for a reason for Chloe's curious behaviour. "Do not refine too much upon it, Lucy, for I dare say Miss Frensham did not mean what she said. We are all a trifle on edge, which is not surprising after the strain of the past few days, and it is very easy to say something which one does not mean. Try to put it out of your mind."

Lucy allowed herself to be mollified. She might have pursued her grievance, but it suddenly occurred to her that Miss Sarah, far from appearing strained, instead looked positively radiant. There could be only one reason for this, and Lucy was singleminded enough, and sufficiently devoted to her mistress, to feel that if the sojourn at the Rose in Hand had brought her and his lordship together, nothing else which had happened there, even the murder of the unfortunate Mr. Bodicote, was of very much importance.

Chloe seemed somewhat subdued for the rest of that day, and once or twice Sarah caught the other woman watching her in a rather furtive, anxious way, as though wondering how much Lucy had told her. Sarah pretended not to notice these doubtful, inquiring glances, but Miss Frensham's oddly inconsistent behaviour continued to puzzle her.

By morning, although slippery slush and overflowing ditches still rendered the going hazardous,

the pike-road was clear enough for vehicles to pass
along it. The first to go by was a mailcoach bound
for Dover, which suggested that conditions might be
better towards London than towards the coast, but
soon after nine o'clock a private carriage coming
from the opposite direction pulled into the yard,
and proved to contain the magistrate and the constable. Mrs. Ashlock greeted Mr. Melchett, to
whom she was well known, with profound relief and
a tearful pouring out of her troubles, but though
he replied sympathetically he refused to be drawn
into a discussion and instead desired her, kindly but
with some firmness, to conduct him to Lord Chayle.

Recalled thus to a sense of what was proper, she
wiped her eyes on the corner of her apron and
ushered him into the parlour, where Justin and
Sarah were sitting. Mr. Melchett seemed surprised
to find himself in the presence of a lady, and when
he had been presented to her and learned that it was
she who had discovered the murdered man, was
very much shocked, so that Justin had no difficulty
in persuading of the desirability of removing Miss
Lorymer to her grandmother's house as soon as she
had given all the information she could. The magistrate agreed at once, saying that he was slightly acquainted with Lady Marlby and would be happy to
call upon Miss Lorymer at Long Fallow Court in
the unlikely event of it proving necessary to question her again. He then qualified this, and dashed
Sarah's hopes of immediate escape from the Rose in
Hand by pointing out regretfully that though the

pike-road was open, the lesser roads and country lanes were still impassable, and that there could be no hope of reaching Clitterbury that day.

Sarah was crestfallen, but she saw that Justin was watching her with some conern, so she did her best to hide her disappointment and dismay. Mr. Melchett then requested her to tell him exactly how she had discovered the body, apologizing for having to ask her anything so disagreeable and assuring her that he would not require her to dwell upon so unpleasant an experience for a moment longer than was necessary.

She did not enjoy telling him, for to do so recalled all too vividly an experience she had been doing her best to forget, and she breathed a sigh of relief when the ordeal was over at last. Justin then told Mr. Melchett of Bodicote's disclosure to him on the day before he died, for he had thought it wiser not to mention this in the letter he had written to the magistrate. Mr. Melchett was very much surprised, giving it as his opinion that this shed a very different light on the affair—though different from what, he omitted to say. Sarah, with a faintly challenging glance at his lordship, ventured to put forward her theory that John Roman and Christopher Frome might be one and the same.

"Lord Chayle does not agree with me, I know," she added, "but I assure you that there are several reasons why I feel that it may very possibly be so."

"I do not entirely disagree," Justin said indulgently. "I have admitted that it is possible, though not very likely. My argument is that, either way, it can have no bearing on Bodicote's death, for a trivial theft, prompted by spite, is a far cry from deliberate murder."

"I fear, ma'am, that I am bound to agree with his lordship," Mr. Melchett agreed apologetically. "This young man may indeed be the thief whom the unfortunate runner was pursuing—that is a question which must be investigated—but however deplorable his behaviour, none of us, I think, can suppose him to be a hardened criminal. I dare say that by now he would like nothing better than to restore the music-box to his uncle and have the whole matter forgotten. Though that, of course, is not for us to decide."

Sarah refrained from pointing out that she had never suggested there might be any connection between the theft and the murder. She had suddenly realized that, setting aside the question of John Roman's identity, Mr. Melchett's inquiries were bound to have unpleasant results for Chloe, who, according to the elder Mr. Frome, was undoubtedly implicated in the theft of the silver music-box. Sarah still felt herself to be deeply in Miss Frensham's debt, and it had occurred to her that a word of warning might not come amiss. Frank answers to the magistrate's questions would perhaps help to make the consequences to Chloe less severe.

Finding that Mr. Melchett had, at present, no more questions to ask her, she excused herself and went out. In the coffee room, Mrs. Ashlock was talking anxiously to Mr. Chebworth, while Toby, who obviously considered that, at present, this was

the most interesting place to be, was curled up un-
obtrusively in the corner of the window-seat with
Tatters sprawled, sleeping, beside him. When Sarah
went into the passage, she saw that the door of the
taproom was open and that the coachman and the
other men, who had been standing talking inside the
room, had paused in their conversation and were all
looking towards the coffee room and the parlour.
She ignored them, and went on along the passage
and up the stairs.

Chloe was not in the big bedroom, and Sarah,
who had expected to find her there, felt somewhat at
a loss. Since her purpose was to offer a confidential
warning, it would not do to go searching for Chloe
about the inn, but if she returned to the parlour it
was unlikely that an opportunity to utter any such
warning would occur.

Uncertain what to do, she walked across to the
window, looked at the singularly uninviting prospect outside, and then turned and somewhat aim-
lessly surveyed the room. She noticed that the quilt
on the fourposter was disarranged over the pillows
at one side, as though whoever made the bed that
morning had done so in a careless, scrambling sort
of way, and being of incurably neat habits herself,
went absently to straighten it. Then she checked,
and stood staring, for protruding from beneath the
pillow, where it had obviously been thrust hastily
out of sight, was a corner of Chloe's blue-kid reticule. The same reticule which, when discovered the
previous day in Lucy's hands, had had so curious
an effect upon its owner.

Very slowly Sarah turned back the coverlet, pulled aside the pillow, and stood frowning down at the reticule. It was somewhat larger than the bags usually carried by fashionably dressed women, though since Chloe was on a journey and might have wished to keep various small items of value with her, this was not surprising. What was puzzling was her reason for trying to hide it, when it had hitherto been carried with her about the inn or left hanging in the cupboard.

Hesitantly Sarah picked it up. It looked bulky and felt unexpectedly heavy, and as she held it between her hands she could feel, through the soft leather, the outline of some hard, rectangular object inside. For a few moments longer she hesitated, then, with sudden decision combined with a degree of reluctance, unfastened the bag and peeped inside.

The grey daylight gleamed dully on metal, and, with a gasp at finding her suspicions so dramatically confirmed, she drew out from the reticule a silver box. Dropping the bag on the bed again, she held the little casket in both hands, turning it this way and that to study the pictures engraved upon it; pictures which, even to her uninformed eyes, were unmistakably Indian in origin. She lifted the lid, and the tinkling notes of a melody sounded sweetly through the room, while within the box the little silver nightingale, exquisitely fashioned, turned gently from side to side, and spread and folded its tiny gleaming wings.

So fascinated by the beauty and ingenuity of this

costly toy that she forgot for the moment the implications of its presence there, Sarah stood holding
the box while the melody ran its course. The notes
were still sounding, though ever more slowly and
faintly, when the door of the room was flung violently open, and John Roman's voice, lowered but
shaking with an unpleasant mingling of anger and
fear, said explosively:

"For God's sake, Chloe! Are you mad? Put that
damned thing away before—!"

The sentence ended abruptly as a couple of paces
into the room brought him to a spot where he could
see that it was Sarah, and not Chloe, who stood by
the bed. For a few heart-stopping seconds they
stared at each other, while the last faint notes of the
little tune, like the fading ghost of a melody, fell
softly into the stillness between them. Then, making
a visible, desperate effort to retrieve a situation
which was, although he did not know it, already
beyond repair, he said with a sneer:

"Prying into Miss Frensham's property, ma'am?
It's not likely you're stealing, so I fancy you're just
indulging in vulgar curiosity. I wonder what Lord
Chayle would say to that."

Quite unexpectedly, Sarah lost her temper, so
that her first alarm was swallowed up by anger. His
words and tone flicked her on the raw, for it
seemed, absurdly, that there was some justification
for them. It was not pleasant to be found searching
someone else's bag, no matter how greatly justified
such search might be.

"Miss Frensham's property?" she retorted scornfully. "I am credibly informed, sir, that this music-box is the property of your uncle, Mr. Frome."

Her words were an even greater shock to him than his unexpected appearance on the scene had been to her, literally staggering him so that he put out a groping hand as though in search of support. A greyish pallor overspread his face and sweat started on his brow as he stared at Sarah in a numb, disbelieving way. His mouth opened and shut several times before any sound emerged, but at last he managed to utter in a strangled voice:

"What did you say?"

"Oh, come now, Mr. Roman—or should I not say, 'Mr. Christopher Frome'? You stole this music-box from your uncle to spite him, and Mr. Bodicote was the Bow Street Runner hired to track you down. If that poor man had not been murdered—!"

The words faltered into silence, for, watching Frome, she saw an odd change come into his face. The stunned look still lingered, but his eyes blazed suddenly with a mixture of terror and fury which was curiously shocking, and in an instant of appalled revelation she realised the truth. This was the murderer. This was how he must have looked at Bodicote when the Runner, shrewder than either she or Justin had supposed, tried to arrest him.

They both moved at the same moment, she making a frantic dart towards the open door, he plunging forward with outstretched arms to stop her. He actually touched her, but the silken folds of the shawl about her shoulders defeated his intention and she twisted free, leaving the shawl in his hands, and gained the passage ahead of him. Still clutching the silver box, she fled towards the stairs, and had reached the top of them when he caught her, his fingers fastening themselves about her throat with such vicious, unexpected strength that the cry she tried to utter became no more than a choking gasp. Instinctively her own hands flew up to try to break that murderous grip, and the music-box dropped from them to go skidding and bouncing down the stairs to crash on to the stone-flagged floor of the passage below.

Sarah, half fainting from fright and from the merciless grip tightening upon her throat, was only dimly aware that, in spite of her feeble struggles, Frome was beginning to drag her back along the upper passage. Then, as though from a great distance, she heard a shout—Justin's voice—footsteps bounding up the stairs two at a time, and she was released so suddenly that she fell in a heap against the wall. There was a flurry of violent movement close at hand, and the sound of a heavy fall, and then she was swept up into a crushing embrace. Justin said, with a note of anguish in his voice which reached even to her failing senses:

"Sarah! Oh, my God!"

The need to reassure him dragged her back from the very brink of unconsciousness, and with a tremendous effort she opened her eyes and looked up into his face, bent close above hers. He was very white, shaken out of his habitual calm composure, and with a look in his usually cool grey eyes which told her more clearly than words how much she had come to mean to him. People were crowding up the stairs and into the passage; alarmed, excited voices exclaimed and questioned, but just at that moment this seemed of no importance at all to either of them. The last barriers had been swept away, and they had finally found each other.

It was Mr. Melchett who ventured to intrude upon them. Coming to stand at Justin's shoulder, where his lordship still knelt with Sarah in his arms, he said anxiously:

"Shocking affair! Shocking! I do trust that Miss Lorymer is not seriously harmed, my lord?"

Sarah, finding speech for the moment impossible, shook her head, and Justin replied, in a voice which was still not entirely steady:

"I think not, though Roman's murderous intention was plain enough. I fancy you need look no farther for Bodicote's killer."

He got up as he spoke and set Sarah on her feet, still keeping his arms around her. Thus comfortingly encircled, she leaned against him and looked apprehensively about. Frome was sitting slumped against the opposite wall with both hands clasped to his head. Joe Ashlock stood threateningly over him, and Chloe was on her knees at his side, dabbing at his mouth with a bloodstained handkerchief. Sarah saw that she was crying. The narrow passage was full of people; Mr. Chebworth; various members of the Ashlock family; Lucy pushing her way anxiously towards her mistress. Sarah swallowed, and said in a painful whisper:

"He *is* Christopher Frome. I found the music-box."

"I know," Justin replied gently. "You dropped it when he attacked you, and it was the sound of it clattering down the stairs which attracted my attention. I do not know what became of it."

"Here it be, my lord." Toby came wriggling importantly between the larger persons of his elders, the silver box in his hand. "I picked it up, but it be all smashed-like. Even the little bird's head's broke off." He checked, peering, and then added with strong excitement: "No, it ain't! It's opened like a little lid, and there's summat inside."

"What's that?" Mr. Melchett started forward. "Here, my boy, give it to me."

Toby handed it over, and the hum of talk died expectantly away as the magistrate, after looking closely at the silver nightingale, poked an experimental finger into its hollow body. He fetched out a scrap of fine silk wrapped around something hard, and a moment later had shaken into the palm of his other hand two magnificent rubies, glowing with rich colour even in the indifferent light of the passage.

"Bless my soul!" he ejaculated, and lifted one of them between finger and thumb. "Bless . . . my . . . soul!"

"So that's it!" Justin said softly. "No wonder the old gentleman was so anxious to recover his property, but why the devil did Frome not take the gems and throw away the box? The fool must have known it could incriminate him."

Chapter XIV

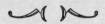

That question was answered an hour or so later, by Chloe. By that time, Christopher Frome was under lock and key in the cellar; Mr. Layton, bewildered but deeply thankful, had been released from his room; and Sarah was settled in an armchair by the parlour fire, the bruises on her neck anointed with a balm of Mrs. Ashlock's providing, and, on a table close by, a soothing drink which the landlady had concocted to ease the soreness of her throat. Justin was sitting beside her, and Mr. Melchett on the opposite side of the fireplace, while between them, facing the fire, Chloe sat, pale and red-eyed, to answer the magistrate's questions.

Yes, she admitted, she had known of the theft of the silver box, but at that time neither she nor Frome had been aware of its secret. After the quarrel he had taken it, as Mr. Bodicote had surmised, out of sheer malice, but, having brought it home and shown it to her, fear of the consequences—for he had always been afraid of his uncle—had overcome him, and he had precipitately left London, taking the box with him, intending to visit a friend of his schooldays who lived in Kent.

"Next morning," Chloe went on, "Mr. Frome came looking for him. He made no secret of it. Said he knew Kit had stolen the box, but it would do him no good because no one would give him more than a fraction of its value. On the other hand, *he* had a great sentimental attachment to it, and if it was returned to him undamaged, he'd say no more about the theft, he'd settle all Kit's debts and give him five hundred pounds besides. At first I pretended to know nothing, but in the end I agreed to try and get word to Kit."

"Without seeking to strike a better bargain?" Justin said caustically. "Chloe, you disappoint me."

She cast him a look of dislike, and addressed her next words exclusively to Mr. Melchett. "I didn't believe his talk of sentiment. From what I could see of him and what Kit had told me, I'd be willing to wager he never had a sentimental thought in his life. If he was willing to pay that much to get the box back, it was more than just a pretty toy. I wrote to Kit, but I told him I'd meet him in Canterbury. Then I packed up and left."

"Followed by the Runner whom Frome had hired to watch you as soon as you agreed to his bargain," Justin put in. "I'm surprised that your estimate of his character did not warn you of the possibility of treachery."

"Why Canterbury?" Mr. Melchett asked hurriedly.

"It was the most convenient place for us to meet. My plan was to go on to Dover and cross from there to France, so that we were out of Frome's reach. On the way we would try to find out what made the box so valuable, and either turn that to good account or make him pay high for its return, whichever offered the greater profit. I had to come by the stage instead of travelling post because we had precious little money for such a journey, but when the damned thing overturned in that drift I wished I'd been less thrifty. Then I found that Kit was stranded here, too, and we agreed it would be safer to pretend to be strangers, especially as Lord Chayle knew me. We were going to leave separately as soon as we were able, and meet again in Dover."

"And you held to that intention, even after Bodicote was murdered?" Mr. Melchett said sternly. "Are you not aware that to do so must implicate you in the guilt of that crime?"

"But I didn't know! I swear I didn't!" Chloe's voice rose; her eyes were wide with alarm. "I thought Layton killed him. I didn't know he was a Runner, and never guessed Kit had any reason to harm him."

Since Frome had already told him the same thing, the magistrate did not pursue the matter any further just then. The young man had broken down completely on realising how he had betrayed himself, and confessed what happened on the night of the murder. Bodicote, who had begun to suspect the truth by keeping a close watch on him and Chloe Frensham, had taken the opportunity, while Frome was at cards with Justin, of searching his room for the music-box, but Frome had come up-stairs sooner than he expected and found him there. The Runner had disclosed his identity and accused him, and Frome, in a fit of blind fury and panic such as had prompted his assault on Sarah, attacked and killed him; then, coming to his senses, he en-deavoured to avert suspicion by hiding the body in the cupboard.

"As to that," Mr. Melchett said now in reply to Chloe's denial, "it will be for the court to decide. You will be taken with Frome to Canterbury and lodged in prison there." He got up and went to the door. "Constable! See that this young woman is confined somewhere secure until I am ready to leave."

"One thing still puzzles me," Justin said reflec-tively. "Why did Frome give the box to you? You were sharing a room with Miss Lorymer and her maid, and you have no baggage with you in which it could be concealed. One would suppose it to be safer with him."

Chloe shrugged. "He said that when inquiries into the murder were made, it might be thought necessary to search the rooms and possessions of all the men here, and that so unusual an object as that music-box would be bound to occasion remark." She glanced at the waiting constable and rose to her feet, turning to Sarah with a faint, wry smile. "Goodbye, Miss Lorymer. Believe me, I'm still grateful for all your kindness, and if it's not an impertinence, I'd like to wish you happy." She glanced at Justin. "You, too, my lord. You're luckier than you deserve."

Mr. Melchett uttered an outraged exclamation and hustled her out of the room, closing the door behind them. Sarah looked at Chayle, and he saw that there were tears in her eyes.

"Oh, Justin, I am so sorry for her! Can nothing be done to help her?"

He reached out to take her hand. " 'Anyone unhappy or in trouble,' " he quoted with a smile. "Very well, my love. I do not know what, if anything, *can* be done, but I promise I will use my best endeavours. For your sake I may add, and not because I feel any sympathy for Chloe Frensham." Then his smile faded and he added abruptly: "Sarah, I cannot forgive myself for what happened to you today. To see you hurt and so badly frightened, and to know that the fault was mine—!"

"Oh, no! How can you say so?" she exclaimed in distress. "It was you who rescued me."

"It was I who put you in danger in the first place," he replied bitterly. "I should have paid more heed to your belief that John Roman was Christopher Frome, instead of brushing it aside as an amusing fancy. I knew that Bodicote was in pursuit of Frome, and the briefest consideration would have shown me that if Roman *were* he, then Roman was the most likely suspect. I mishandled the whole affair from beginning to end, and you had to suffer for my folly. Had Melchett not decided when he did to inspect the cupboard where Bodicote was found, we should have known nothing of your danger until it was too late."

Sarah moved from her chair to seat herself on his lordship's knee, slipping her arm round his neck and laying her cheek against his. Such boldness would have horrified Mama, but Sarah had resolved never again to be influenced by Mama's advice where Justin was concerned.

"I will not permit you to blame yourself so absurdly," she said softly. "If I had kept my wits about me when he found me with the music-box, I could have found a way to evade him and come to you and Mr. Melchett for help." She sat upright and looked at him with a rueful smile creeping into her eyes. "The truth is that he said something which made me lose my temper, and you were quite right. I did not stop to think. Before I knew what was happening I had let slip all I knew about him. His real name, his uncle, Mr. Bodicote—everything! What happened was entirely my own fault, so please, can we not forget it, and not speak of it any more? After all, Mr. Melchett thought my suspicions absurd, too."

His arms tightened around her. "Generous as well as warmhearted," he said wryly. "Very well, we'll say no more about it, though I shall continue to hold myself very much to blame." A tentative knocking sounded on the door, and he added impatiently: "Devil take it! Are we never to be free of interruption?"

Sarah sighed, but slipped from his hold and re-

turned demurely to her own chair. Justin, rising,
said, "Come in," and the sallow, bony countenance
of Mr. Layton peered hesitantly into the room.

"My most humble apologies, my lord, for intrud-
ing," he said nervously, "but may I beg the favour
of a word with your lordship?"

"By all means," Justin said resignedly, "but pray
come in, Mr. Layton, and close the door."

Thus encouraged, Layton obeyed, bowed profoundly to Sarah, and addressed himself apologetically to Chayle.

"I hesitate to trouble you, my lord, but the case
is desperate. Since I am no longer under suspicion,
and the road is now passable, the magistrate tells me
that I am free to go on my way, and it is imperative
that I should do so without delay. Unhappily, Ashlock informs me that he keeps no horses for hire,
and he will not lend me his own to ride to the posting house because someone would then have to
walk to the village to fetch it back."

He paused, looking pathetically at Justin who,
torn between amusement and vexation, said coolly:

"You have my sympathy, sir, but I fail to see
how I may assist you. Perhaps Mr. Melchett will
take you up with him as far as the village."

"There is no room," Layton explained dolefully.
"He has the constable with him, and now there are
two prisoners to be conveyed to Canterbury. I have
begged him to allow me the use of Roman's horse,
but he will not hear of it, even though—" a faintly
aggrieved note crept into his voice "—the animal
will have to be removed from this place sooner or

later. I thought that perhaps your lordship would condescend to have a word with him on my behalf. I would not presume to trouble you, but I *must* go on my way. I have been looked for in Dover these five days past."

"I fear you overrate my influence with Mr. Melchett," Justin replied, "and if he does not consider it proper to give you the use of the horse, it is not likely that anything I may say will alter his opinion. I believe, however, that some reparation is due to you for the unpleasantness of the last few days, and I am quite willing to point this out to him if you wish."

Mr. Layton started to thank him but suddenly broke off, a look of horror spreading over his face. For the past minute or two there had been sounds of activity in the stable yard, succeeded by footsteps and voices as the new arrival entered the coffee room, and now one of these voices, a female tone of startling power and volume, was heard to remark:

"In there, is he? Then out of my way, young woman, for I've a score to settle, and I've come a long way to do it."

A protest from Polly Ashlock was not attended to, and the parlour door was flung violently open, revealing a middle-aged woman of formidable proportions and commanding aspect. An unfashionable pelisse of good, dark cloth was buttoned tightly over her massive bosom; a bonnet, severely unadorned, framed iron-grey hair and a fleshy, uncompromising face with an exceedingly hard mouth. Perceiving the cringing Mr. Layton, this apparition flung out an accusing hand and ejaculated, in a tone of mingled triumph and menace:

"Ha!"

She then surged forward into the room, nodded curtly to the astonished Sarah and Justin, folded her arms and fixed Layton with a gorgon-like glare.

"So there you are, you miserable little toad!" she greeted him. "Thought you'd got away, didn't you? Thought I didn't know about your visits to Dover, and the young widow with a snug little business there you're planning to marry the day after tomorrow? Well, you're wrong—on both counts! I do know, and it's my girl you'll be marrying, and no one else. My girl, that you've wronged and deserted."

"Madam!" Justin had recovered a little from his astonishment, and after directing a quelling glance at his betrothed, who was showing a lamentable tendency to giggle, addressed the intruder with glacial courtesy. "Since your business with Mr. Layton would appear to be peculiarly delicate, permit me to suggest that you conduct it elsewhere—in private."

"Oh?" The basilisk glare was turned upon him. "And who may you be, and what concern is it of yours?"

"My name, ma'am, is Chayle, and since this happens to be a private room, I fear I must request that you leave it."

"If it's a private room," she demanded triumphantly, "what's *he* doing here?"

"Mr. Layton, ma'am, is here at my invitation,"

he replied freezingly. "Is it necessary for me to point out that you are not?"

She ignored the latter words. "Then you'd best know the sort of scoundrel you've been inviting. A deceiver, Mr. Chayle! A wicked seducer of innocent maidens! But he'll do right by my girl. I'll see to that. He'll make a poor sort of son-in-law, but I won't have my first grandchild coming in by a side door, with no right to its father's name."

"Upon my soul, did you ever hear the like?" Mrs. Ashlock, summoned by the frantic Polly, appeared suddenly in the doorway. "I'll thank you, my good woman, to keep a decent tongue in your head, and to come out of that parlour this minute. Talking like that in front of a young lady, and being uncivil to his lordship—I don't know what things are coming to, and that's a fact! You come back to the public rooms, or I'll call the constable to put you out."

Mr. Layton's nemesis swung round to face her, clearly prepared to do battle with Mrs. Ashlock as well as everyone else, but since Layton was taking advantage of the momentary wandering of her attention by endeavouring to sidle out of the room, she uttered another awe-inspiring exclamation and swept in pursuit. Mrs. Ashlock looked at Justin, sought in vain for words, then threw up her hands in a helpless gesture and withdrew, closing the door behind her.

The latch had barely clicked before Sarah collapsed into helpless laughter. Justin, his own eyes bright with amusement, regarded her with mock severity.

"There is nothing whatsoever to laugh at. Besides being so grossly improper that you should not have understood a word of it, if what that appalling woman said was true, Layton is a thoroughly unprincipled scoundrel."

"But it is so absurd!" Sarah gasped, dabbing her eyes with a handkerchief. "Everyone feeling so certain he was trying to escape because he was the murderer, when all the while—! Oh, Justin, can you wonder that he was in such desperate haste to go on his way?"

"Not in the least! The prospect of acquiring such a mother-in-law would be enough to terrify any man. I cannot help feeling that however badly Layton has behaved, he will be more than adequately punished for it."

"Yes, indeed! He will never know one peaceful moment. You know, I cannot help feeling just a little sorry for him."

"No!" Justin spoke very firmly, though with a tremor of laughter in his voice. "I forbid it absolutely. For Chloe I will do what I can, but not even for you, my darling, will I endeavour to save Layton from his just deserts at the hands of that terrifying female. One encounter with the lady was more than enough."